FABIAN
A CUBIST BIOGRAPHY
TOM NEWTON
RECITAL

For Frazer and Reya

Contents

FOREWORD

I HAVE ALWAYS FELT ambivalent about biographies. Even the most diligent biographer, after months of meticulous research, is still dependent on the memories and reports of others. Fiction seems more honest; it makes no claims to truth and objectivity.

That aside, I also find myself attracted to them. It is human nature to wonder about human nature—about what it is like to be another person, to feel their thoughts, desires, and motivations, to be curious about their deeds.

The subjects of biographies invariably tend to be people who are regarded as important and are quite often deceased. Would readers of such books be aroused by a biography of a wet nurse, or a wainwright?

That fascination with important people might be a vicarious way to rise from the bubbling mass of humanity and stand on a pinnacle, even if it is someone else's pinnacle. Biography might be the literary expression of such instincts.

These conflicting views inspired me to attempt a biography of sorts, although I knew its subject would have to be a fictitious character, as I am myself.

Tom Newton
Woodstock, New York
1837

"Things are not what they seem. They just seem to be what they are."

Dr Paul French, MD

Chapter 1

I wanted to write a biography of someone who had never lived—someone who came into existence through me, but without any interference from my mind—a person I knew as little about as someone I had never met. It would be an almost immaculate conception. I say 'almost' because I would have to be involved, at least initially.

Biographers are expected to be objective. They put a lot of time and effort into researching their subjects. To do research on someone who does not exist is problematic, or virtually impossible, a task better left to a novelist.

I decided that astrology would be a good option. Using a horoscope I could create a character I knew nothing about simply by interpreting a chart. I would still have to come up with the annoying necessities of name, date and place of birth but after that my role would be secretarial.

I chose the name Charles Michael Brown. It was not particularly remarkable. There must have been millions who shared that name and none of them had asked to be born. I may have just referred to an immaculate conception but what appealed to me more was an immaculate existence, where things came into being fully formed like alchemical homunculi. If that were to be the case I would never have had to write this fictitious biography in the first place, because it would already have been written.

January 20th, 1920, 5:47 am. I hoped that my character would not be anyone special. I was tired of history dominated by celebrity. It is unfortunate that those not considered to have done anything are forgotten, as if they'd never lived. But now at least I had the date and time of birth.

I would have to try to remember that Mr. Brown was not my character. I didn't want to be one of those writers who are possessive of their characters while at the same time claiming they act independently. I was just the instrument that facilitated his birth into a fictitious life. All I needed was a place.

Staines, England. I didn't know it. I knew of it. I might have even been there once or twice. I felt that Staines was the perfect place in 1920 for Charles Michael Brown to have been born—right after the First World War, a time of some turmoil.

I got a chart online in a few seconds for free, without having to plough through ephemerides, although its interpretation was another matter. It was not important to me whether I believed in astrology or not. I had found a way to use it as a tool.

I would use my shoe as a hammer and nail the horoscope to the wall. I watched it emerge from the printer. The network of lines crossing the circle confused me. They apparently denoted the aspects. I was about to undertake something I was not sure I still wanted to do. Having an idea is all very well. Its implementation is something else.

This might be a flaw in my personality, a square on my chart. I was never able to summon enough motivation to participate in those long cross-country runs that were required of me when I was young. I was more inclined to smoke hashish beneath the railway bridge while listening to the clumping feet overhead. When I had counted a suitable and convincing number of bodies, I would emerge surreptitiously, roll a little in the mud and stagger across the finish line, fulfilling what was demanded of me. Some people might regard this as laziness or a lack of self-discipline. Others might see it as an act of rebellion by a spirit that would not be shackled to bovine conformity. It was such an ambiguity that led me to write this false biography, if it could in fact be called a biography.

I was beginning to have my doubts about the name Charles Michael Brown. Fabian Davis kept drifting around my head, with the middle initial L. It might stand for Lewis—possibly a recurring name in the family on the maternal side. Or maybe it was an initial with darker implications, like Lear—Fabian Lear Davis. That was better. But I feared that he would no longer be the everyman I had hoped for. I had set out to completely remove myself from anything I would write but already I wanted to influence the story.

Chapter 2

Fabian's father was a senior officer in the middle management level of the Civil Service. Every day he took the train to the city and every night he ensconced himself in his study. He was a firm believer in hierarchies, a strict but non-violent authoritarian. The business of tending to children fell squarely into his wife's domain as far as he was concerned, and his own concerns were paramount in his household.

I have not been able to ascertain from the chart whether Fabian had siblings. My intuition tells me that he was an only child. His mother was the daughter of a Presbyterian minister—Robert Lear Alexander. A dour fanatic. Fabian never knew him but he didn't need to. The effects of this man rippled across generations, first numbing the mother, who in turn affected her son through her distance from him. I know this because of the position of the moon in Capricorn, Fabian's natal sign. That lack of closeness in a relationship between mother and child—a relationship which is supposed to be close and loving, at least by our contemporary western standards, is potentially a rich literary vein. That word—vein—makes me think of mining.

People have been doing it for years, digging holes in mountains, shoring up narrow passageways with rickety timbers. It was always a risky affair, full of suffering, danger, disease, noxious gases, rock falls and canaries. All in the name of extraction, carried out by people mostly forgotten by history and usually anonymous. Everything they dug up was dubious—as what real value pertains to metal?

Fabian was destined to travel, but that would be in the future, after the Second World War. There is nothing particularly mysterious about this. It has more of a certain robotic inevitability, programmed by the stars for the sake of convenience.

He was extremely ambitious in a calculating way. To most people he seemed affable, with the gift of the gab and very persuasive, but on a deeper level, which was rarely perceptible, he was cold and quite ruthless. The evidence of this is written in his chart. Everything I know about the sun leads me to believe that it is hot, but apparently the sun in Capricorn may suggest a cold and calculating personality. Astrology, like most things, is rife with contradiction but I am beginning to see the advantage of contradiction. It has a quality of attraction and repulsion like the poles of a magnet, a dynamism that ensures the world is never static.

Perhaps astrology arose because the moon could be seen to affect the tides and so the other planets would have their own influences as well. Or it might be a vestige of ancient thinking, some old impulse buried in one of those ancestral brain layers that has a name like 'Reptilian', except that astrology is not reptilian. It belongs somewhere else—The Sidereal Brain, the logic of the stars. An identification with the heavens, where the planetary bodies were associated with organs of the human body, meant that Fabian would be susceptible to orthopaedic problems due to his sun sign being Capricorn.

A dark force is at work in all this sidereal reality—the force of gravity, so hard to understand. My favourite description of it at the moment is of space bearing down. It is a more satisfying explanation than that things fall because the ground is their rightful place.

Chapter 3

I am curious whether floor covering could be influential in shaping a person's life. A young child spends a lot of time on the floor, or close to it, and it is a common opinion that early childhood experiences have a lasting effect. I wonder about this because Staines was the site of the world's first linoleum factory, set up in 1864 by its inventor Frederick Walton and functional up until the 1950s. So linoleum was ever present in Fabian's childhood and like many other households of the time, the Davis family residence at 64 High Street was done out with it in the hallway and kitchen. I am trying to find a concrete explanation for Fabian's later interest in travel. Venus in Sagittarius and Jupiter in Leo imply an interest in foreign cultures and religions to some extent, but I am looking for an earthbound explanation, something through which the planetary influences might manifest themselves.

The answer could be linoleum. I imagine that the materials it is made from might affect humans.

Apparently the majority of Americans have a chemical in their blood that was used as a propellant for rocket fuel. It probably seeped into the groundwater in the 1950s, right about the time when the influence of linoleum waned. So there was an overlap of toxicities. Frederick Walton was the instigator of the first and Jack Parsons the second, who aside from getting government contracts for his work on rocket fuel and jet-propelled takeoff, led a double life of drug use and sex magic. He blew himself up in his laboratory. It might have been suicide, or it might have been murder. Perhaps it was just an accident. I don't know what became of Mr. Walton.

From the late nineteenth century up until the mid-twentieth, a growing number of people could have been contaminated by cork dust, linoxyn and pine rosin, with perhaps some benzene. It might of course be utter nonsense. It's just a thought that occurred to me. The effect of the rocket fuel propellant on the population is unknown though it might be linked to a depreciation in intelligence. One of the many interesting things about Jack Parsons was that he was defrauded of his life savings by his girlfriend and L. Ron Hubbard, who ran off together.

Whether Fabian had been affected by linoleum or not, his childhood was lonely. His parents were emotionally unconcerned with him. From an early age he spent a lot of time in boarding school where the duties of parenting were delegated to a system. But despite the loneliness Fabian had a cheerful demeanour and was popular among his classmates. His natural intelligence enabled him to glide through his schoolwork seemingly without effort. Only later, in his adolescence, did he notice a state of dissatisfaction within himself. His achievements gave him no lasting pleasure but only inspired him to accomplish more, in the hope perhaps that satisfaction was attainable. This is suggested by the Sun and Moon in Capricorn. Venus in the Twelfth House seems to provide his resilience against loneliness. Fabian was both introverted and gregarious.

As a young boy he read a lot. He particularly enjoyed the Victorian children's novels by E. Nesbit. Serendipitously, while doing my cursory research, I discovered that E. Nesbit was a founder of the Fabian Society, a socialist organisation that was later connected to the Labour Party. This coincidence of the same name is a lovely and unexpected strand of the web. It shows me that even though Fabian's story is manifested through me, it actually extends far beyond.

CHAPTER 4

When he was fifteen Fabian saw the film *The 39 Steps*, which had just come out. He liked to say that this film was a turning-point in his life. It was an epiphany for him. As he left the cinema he knew that he wanted to make films. It is likely that this is an embroidery of the truth, a constructed narrative to suit the persona he desired to project. There is nothing true about Fabian. True or not, he began to develop an interest in films at that time. He was familiar with John Buchan's book *The Thirty-Nine Steps* and was fascinated by how Alfred Hitchcock had turned it into a film. The letters in the title had become numbers. He saw this as an example of the artistic benefits of technology, and the gears of his ambition were engaged. He was to become a film director. Fabian knew nothing about filmmaking but that did not discourage him. His patience was unlimited. He did not care how long it took. It would in fact be only six years before he found himself looking out from behind a camera—sooner than he had expected.

He kept his new ambition to himself. His parents would not have approved. Arthur Davis thought a career in accounting, or ideally a position in The Civil Service was the obvious direction he should take. His mother Virginia didn't care but would not have approved of anything he said he wanted to do. So he spent the next six years plotting and trying to teach himself about film making, which meant reading everything he could get his hands on about the subject, which was not much. Later he was influenced by Eisenstein's *Film Form* and *Film Sense*. He also went to the cinema as much as he could, sometimes going back to see the same film many times. He found that with multiple viewings his initial emotional involvement fell away leaving him able to dispassionately observe how the film was put together.

Ironically he would have made a good accountant or civil servant. He had the brain and temperament for it, as Mercury in Capricorn conjunct to the Moon makes clear. But these influences were offset by both Neptune and Jupiter in Leo in the Eighth House, which among other things suggest an affinity for arts and entertainment.

At university he got involved with the theatre and when he became friends with Helen, a fellow student, she introduced him to the films of Dali and Bunuel—*L'Age d'Or* and *Un Chien Andalou*. Helen was interested in Modern Art. Most of it was happening across the Channel in Paris at the time. They talked about going there. The Bunuel-Dalí films opened up a new realm of possibilities for Fabian, widening his awareness of what he could do and taking him beyond the dramas of suspense that had enthralled him. Portraying life as a dream-state made all kinds of directions possible. He still liked suspense but realised that it did not have to be rooted in an orthodox perception of reality. The surrealist films were not particularly suspenseful, relying more on the strategy of shock. The images of the blade across the eyeball, the donkey hauling the piano and the ants crawling from a wounded palm were shocking indeed, but they also struck him as brittle in a way. They did not have the depth or irony of drama. Shock always requires more shock as the audience becomes inured to it, and is therefore ultimately unfulfilling. He also felt there was a certain self-righteousness to these films, as if the director assumed he knew better, or more, than other people. Fabian suspected that no one really knew anything. There was no room for self-righteousness in the world. It was a piece of wisdom one might normally have associated with an older person. Luis Bunuel might have been shocked himself, to find his films appreciated by the sequacious bourgeoisie he was trying to insult.

As the stars have shown, Fabian was very focused and ambitious. He knew what he wanted and pursued it with tact but without compromise, though he never assumed that his ideas were the only valid or correct ones. They pertained to himself. Other people had just the same right to their different opinions as he did.

One evening at a pub in Cambridge he was involved in a conversation about the theory of relativity. Simon Beale was reading physics and took it on himself to explain Einstein's theory to a gaggle of would-be thespians and literature students. Simon was enjoying his position of superior knowledge but he was also a good teacher. Despite his clear explanations, most of what he said went over Fabian's head, except for one phrase—'extended present'. The juxtaposition of those two words excited him without even knowing what was meant and he perked up. Before that he had been distracted by a game of shove ha'penny. He had been trying to think of all the different names for the ancient game: shoffe-groat, shovilla-bourde, slide thrift, slype-grote and then—'extended present'. His attention had snapped back.

"Most people understand time as what has happened, what is happening now and what will happen—past, present, and future. But Einstein's special theory of relativity shows that this is not the case. There is an intermediate state, neither past nor future—the extended present. Its duration increases with distance from the observer. At close up, that duration is so short it cannot be perceived by human senses. But if you were to observe an event in a precise moment of time from the Moon, the extended present would last a few seconds and if you went further out to Mars, it would be fifteen minutes. So in this moment that you think of as NOW, some things would have already happened and others would be yet to come. A moment cannot be objectively perceived or described."

Fabian was floored. There is no such thing as now. That is the way he saw it. The realisation was thrilling. It had the ring of poetry and stayed with him always. No sooner had it sunk in than he began to explore ways he could use the idea.

In a general sense, film suggested a linear progression of time. Footage of celluloid passed from one spool to another, in camera and projector, each frame moving sequentially through the gate. There was no movement of the images themselves. Only the medium that contained the still images moved. It was an archaic trick like the zoetrope. It seemed a crude mechanism when compared to the concept of the extended present. If one slowed or stopped the film running through the projector, causing the film to melt and the screen to portray bubbling celluloid, could that represent the extended present? Not really. It might be better achieved by having two actors experience a different duration of the same scene. He could imagine filming an actor who sat in a cinema watching the screen on which he was portrayed sitting in the cinema and watching the screen but that was more Escher than extended present. It was a difficult concept to express visually.

In the future the process of film making would be much more sophisticated. Celluloid would no longer be needed. The images themselves might move, just like reality. Cameras would be no different than eyes. They would have perception. Fabian was naturally inclined to technology and things mechanical, as Uranus in the Second House and Mars in the Ninth might attest.

Chapter 5

Fabian grew up in turbulent times, as does everyone because all times are turbulent. The only modifier being one's proximity to a turbulent zone and its intensity. As the motions toward war began to fester in Europe, he was enjoying himself at university. It was probably the first protracted period of enjoyment in his life, a newfound liberty from the drabness and solitude of his childhood, which up until then he had considered the normal state of affairs. He had only lived a fraction of his life—most of it was still ahead of him. Hope and excitement were a matter of course.

So Fabian was not unduly concerned with the impending war. He had been relatively unscathed by the Great Depression due to his father's dry but steady employment in the mid to upper rungs of the Civil Service.

It was perhaps due to his father's irrational and implacable hatred of the Irish that he immersed himself in the tales of Irish myth, the stories of Cuchulainn being his favourite.

Cuchulainn was born with the name Sétanta. His mother was Deichtine, the sister or daughter of Conchobar Mac Nessa, the king of Ulster. His father was the god Lugh. There are different versions of the story of his birth. They all involve a group of Ulster men out hunting for magical birds when they are forced to take shelter from a sudden snowstorm. In one version Deichtine rides with them, in another she is the wife of the man who hosts them for the night, presumably the god Lugh. Either way, she becomes pregnant and gives birth to Sétanta.

What immediately strikes me about this are the magical birds—the common thread between the different versions. They become a metaphor, just hinted at, an undercurrent of birds. It makes me think there should be subterranean stories written beneath this one, like a succession of ancient cities that lie beneath each other, deeper and deeper into the past. It would be built from symbols rather than words. Images of birds perhaps.

Those birds would have to fly at such a great depth, that they would barely be noticeable. How would they connect with the story on the surface? It would have to be a courtship, playful and coy. The different stories must desire each other.

Chulainn was a smith whose house was guarded by a ferocious dog. Sétanta killed it in self-defence and when Chulainn was upset about it, Sétanta had to take its place until a suitable canine replacement could be found. Thenceforth, he was known as Cuchulainn—Chulainn's hound. He had black hair. In other versions of the story he was blond, or had hair which was brown, red and yellow in different layers. Fabian liked to think of him with dark hair. He had black hair himself and piercing blue eyes, like a Siberian Husky. People found them shocking to look at, attractive yet vaguely repellent. One's gaze kept returning to them, along with the desire to look away. Fabian's eyes gave him an edge.

He had other similarities with the hero. Both were handsome, diminutive in stature, boyish in appearance, beardless, and had many lovers. Cuchulainn was renowned for his extreme battle frenzy. The tendons in his neck would bunch up into great knots bigger than babies' heads. One eye would come out of its socket and rest on his cheek, the other would be sucked back into his skull. His lungs and kidneys were visible in his throat. He would kill everything in sight, friend or foe. It made no difference. It took scores of women baring their breasts in front of him to distract him long enough to allow the other men to cool him off in successive barrels of water.

This was where their similarities ceased. When Fabian was at school he had to do mandatory military training in the cadet forces for several hours each Wednesday afternoon. Every now and then, that meant bayonet practice. The boys would be lined up on the edge of a field. When the command to fix bayonets came, they twisted their mean seventeen-inch blades onto the ends of their rifles in the prescribed manner and stood at attention. Then one-at-a-time they would be called upon to run twenty yards across the field towards an upright bale of hay. They were instructed to emit blood curdling screams as they ran. When they reached the target they would thrust the bayonet into the bale, twist it to the right and left, then putting a foot against the hay-belly they would pull out the blade and run back.

Despite his best efforts, Fabian's blood curdling screams were never more than whimpers. He was not to be a hero. This was the result of Mars in Libra. He hated confrontation and always fell back on persuasion and tact to further his aims.

The Irish stories offered him relief from Graeco-Roman thought. The Romans never reached Ireland. Irish logic was different from Roman logic. It had been mitigated by Christian missionaries perhaps, but had still managed to maintain some independence. He was sceptical of such opinions even when they were his own. They would have to be proven true and the proofs required for that would have to be proven themselves, and so on, a never ending requirement of proof.[1]

Despite his grace and intelligence, Fabian was so private about his inner feelings, even to himself, that it was almost as if he didn't have any. It would take years for him to open up. But that kind of extreme reserve was cultural for a man of his time and class, raised in an all male boarding school.

The famous exchange between Lord Uxbridge and The Duke of Wellington at the moment that Uxbridge was hit in the leg by a cannon shot, sums it up perfectly even if it never happened: "By God, sir, I've lost my leg!" says Uxbridge. Wellington replies "By God, sir, so you have!"

The amputated limb became a tourist attraction in the village of Waterloo in Belgium.

---

1. This is an example of the regressive argument in epistemology. It is one part of the Münchausen trilemma, which seeks to demonstrate the impossibility of proving any truth. The other two parts of the trilemma are circular argument and dogmatic argument.

Chapter 6

During the summer of 1938 Fabian began to experiment with sensory deprivation. He wanted to discover what would happen if he limited the capacity of one or more of his senses. He started by blocking his ears and going for long walks. He repeated the experiment blocking both his ears and his nose. He felt a sensation of separation and slightly heightened awareness that he found strangely relaxing. His eyes seemed to be working overtime, making up for the loss of the other senses, scanning back and forth much more frequently than usual. Next he added a blindfold in conjunction with the ear and nose plugs. While walking deaf and blind and unable to smell on the beach at Durdle Door in Dorset, he stumbled and fell on some rocks. His right knee took the main impact of the fall and was badly twisted. He was unable to walk and had to wait several hours until some passers-by carried him off the beach. It took a long time for the knee to heal, which it never completely did. At certain times and in certain positions it would give him excruciating pain.

As he lay on his back on the beach, having decided not to attempt getting up again for a while, he removed his blindfold and noticed a gull soaring on a thermal above him, transcribing wide curves in the sky. The gull was green with a red breast, so it could not be a gull. He could see it clearly, circling above him. Everything seemed so unnaturally vivid—the pain in his leg, the bird in the sky. He thought perhaps that this was due to his muted senses being reawakened but that did not seem enough to describe the vibrant reality around him.

The memory of that experience stayed with him. He wanted to know what kind of bird he had seen. It looked like a parrot,[1] not something you would expect above the coastline of southern England in those days. After poring over books in the library he determined that he had seen a quetzal. This was even more unlikely than a parrot.

Though his memory was clear, he could not be sure that what he remembered was what he had actually seen. This vision may have been a result of his injury, or of the prolonged childhood exposure to the noxious vapours of linoleum. Whatever the cause, it left him slightly changed.

He no longer completely trusted his perceptions. He had always taken them for granted. Now he didn't. He took it as a personal failure that he couldn't make sense of what he thought he had seen. He was looking for significance and trying to understand why

---

1. Though there have been reports of feral parrots in the United Kingdom since the mid-nineteenth century, large numbers were not sighted until the late 1990s, so it is very unlikely that Fabian saw a parrot on the south coast of England in 1938.

he needed to find it. He also had to appreciate the possibility of insignificance.

Chapter 7

In 1940 Fabian's education was cut short when he was called up. Due to the condition of his right knee, the examining army medical officer found him unfit for active duty—temporarily at least. His case was to be reviewed at a later date. Instead of the army, Fabian found himself despatched to the newly re-established Ministry of Information. He was assigned to The Crown Film Unit in The Films Division headed by Sir Kenneth Clark.[1] He showed up for his first day of work with a walking stick.

For most people war was a disaster. For Fabian it turned out to be an opportunity. Being declared unfit for duty had been a blow to his self esteem at first but he wasn't bothered for long. He wanted to make films. He had no interest in fighting and couldn't believe

---

1. Sir Kenneth Mackenzie Clark OM CHKCB FBA, 1903-1983, was a British art historian, author, museum director and broadcaster. He was the director of the Ashmolean Museum in Oxford for three years and the director of the National Gallery for twelve. He was also Surveyor of the King's pictures for King George V, a position he held for ten years. He is most widely known for his television programme *Civilisation*, which he wrote and presented.

his luck to have landed in The Films Division. This was going to be the education he had always craved. It was very strange that his damaged knee, still so painful, had made it possible. The beneficial result of his accident felt like destiny. He was not particularly fond of that term but couldn't help wondering why he had been so fortunate. It felt as if his life had been pre-written and mapped out. He had no alternative but to follow where it led.

The Ministry was a shambles, a large, ungainly institution whose remit was bitterly contested. The prospect of one governmental organisation controlling all aspects of information in the British Isles and overseas territories seemed to many to be more in line with their foe across the North Sea than with the English culture they were trying to defend. The Films Division had its own culture, Fabian thought, though his fantasies of rising rapidly to the top were soon tempered by the vacuous reality of the inconsequential paperwork he was assigned—something more suited to his father, but he kept his hopes up.

Shortly after Fabian had started working at the Ministry, Sir Kenneth gave a speech to his underlings and announced that he would be stepping aside to focus on his work recruiting and managing war-artists. Jack Beddington would be taking over his position. Sir Kenneth spoke highly of him and praised his work for Shell before the war, in particular the advertising posters he had commissioned from modern artists. Sir Kenneth was also head of the National Gallery and had just had all the paintings removed and hidden to keep them safe from bombs. He believed that art should be available to all people from all walks of life and now that the paintings had gone, he had to find something to do with the building that would further that aim. He was later approached by the pianist, Myra Hess, who suggested that the empty gallery be used as a concert venue. All the music venues in London had been closed to avoid the risk of mass casualties but Sir Kenneth liked the idea and was able to get Governmental permission, and she organised concerts there throughout the war, to much acclaim.

The Crown Film Unit was responsible for newsreels and public information films. They would also be making documentaries and some feature films. Scripts were already under consideration, including a few written by the poet Dylan Thomas.

Fabian was living with his parents in Staines at the time, and would take the train into London every day. The Ministry was located in Senate House in Bloomsbury. The newly constructed building had been taken over from the University of London. Fabian loved Bloomsbury. It had an atmosphere of literary and artistic brilliance. As he limped through the streets and squares he could feel it, as if it somehow permeated the buildings.

The British Museum was situated in Bloomsbury and it soon became his custom to visit it daily during his lunch hour. He had hoped to look at the Elgin Marbles, which he had seen as a child before the war, but discovered they had been removed for safekeeping. Just in time it turned out, as the bombs started to fall and the museum was hit.

The war which up until then had only seemed to him some distant theoretical event, came rushing in with a vengeance. Nights were full of incarnadine flames and poisonous billowing smoke, illuminated by further explosions and the roving searchlights of the ack-ack guns. The people huddled for safety below ground on station platforms like troglodytes.

By day it was business as usual. He would find his way to work, skirting the cordoned-off areas where crews sifted through piles of rubble still smouldering in the morning light. Day by day he would learn of people he had known who had died. Simon Beale was among them, the student who had introduced him to the special theory of relativity, who disappeared in the sky above London, alone in his Spitfire.

The workload at the Ministry was increasing. Fabian was taken away from his clerical duties and allowed into the editing rooms. At first he was put to menial tasks—fetching film reels, cleaning, bringing tea to the editors. Soon his eagerness and aptitude were noticed and he was rewarded with lessons in editing from the most respected professionals in the industry at the time. He learned quickly.

After that, Fabian's rise gained momentum. It was drawn to Mr Beddington's attention that there was a rare talent among them, albeit young and inexperienced. He was taught how to operate a camera and the rudiments of lighting. Every new field he was introduced to, he tackled with competence and diligence, always displaying alacrity and cheerfulness. His slight and youthful figure, leaning on a cane, which seemed incongruous with his age, and his piercing blue eyes brimming with intelligence and ambition, endeared him to his mentors. They soon came to regard him as a natural—someone who was going to become someone. They might well have seen in him the person they wished they had been themselves. Little did they know the desperation that roiled him and his dissatisfaction with every accomplishment. Nor were they aware of his growing arrogance commensurate with his success—the fallacy of believing that this was all his due. He kept such things well hidden, as was his nature. He was able to see through his own arrogance, but that did not prevent him from feeling it.

In some cases a naïf might be successful because ignorance of what he does not know allows him self-confidence, which in turn convinces more knowledgeable people who are aware of their short-comings and whose confidence is therefore lacking. This was not the case with Fabian. He was well educated and well read. He had a dogged thoroughness that examined every detail. He was aware of what he did not know, but enthusiasm and ambition swept his doubts aside. He knew that in order to make films he must learn every aspect of the craft. Those aspects were clearly defined, so it was easy for him to angle his way from one to another. All he needed for advancement was to play the required political games, and Uranus being in Aquarius made this come quite naturally to him.

The position of Neptune in Leo gave him an eye for famous people. He was attracted to flamboyant and dramatic characters who had capitalised on their idiosyncrasies and basked in public adulation. In turn, they were often drawn to his magnetic if dispassionate personality. He had the opportunity to meet such people—actors, artists, composers, writers and also professionals from behind the camera—cinematographers, producers and directors. They all passed through the Ministry, and with their eagerness to help, most of them had forgotten the distinction between art and propaganda.

At twenty, Fabian was promiscuous, despite his bad knee. The edifice of Victorian morality was beginning to crumble, aided perhaps by the nightly bombing raids which eroded certainty.

He was not religious, being an atheist who occasionally veered towards agnosticism. The fervour of his ancestors made Christianity extremely unattractive to him and the dull Church of England services, obligatory at school, were more concerned with tradition than anything else. And what a tradition! He could never understand why a god from the Middle East held so much sway in Northern Europe. It seemed ridiculous. He was more interested in the religious beliefs of other cultures. He wasn't averse to mysticism either, after his experience at Durdle Door.

According to Helen, Fabian's promiscuity was not so much a youthful hedonism but a search for monogamy. He was looking for a deep connection with someone else and not finding it, so he had to keep trying. If she was right, then there was an irony at work, for the connection he craved was right in front of him and he kept turning away. Unlike many youthful friendships, this one lasted a lifetime, never dissipating. She did not begrudge him his philandering, or even disapprove of it. She was no firm advocate of monogamy herself, believing people should do as they wanted, but Fabian's myopia meant for her a limiting of possibility. As far as he was concerned, whenever he thought about marriage or a relationship with just one person, he remembered his parents with their silent hostility. It was a silence so toxic that it poisoned the very house they inhabited.

Chapter 8

Helen was now a WAAF and spent many hours pushing small planes around on a large map table with something resembling a croupier's rake. She lived in a bed-sit in Earls Court. He would stay with her occasionally, especially when the air-raids made it difficult to get home to Staines.

It was a grim abode. Amenities were pared down to essentials. A single bed stretched beneath the sole window in the room, not an ideal placement as there was a constant draft and dampness that made them cold at night. The floor was covered in a worn and yellowed linoleum. There was a small gas fire against one wall but it was ineffective as a heat source. They had to huddle in front of it at a distance of six to twelve inches, and there was only room for one person at a time. They would take turns to toast bread on a fork in front of it. The room always smelt faintly of gas.

There was an impersonal nature to the place. It was just somewhere to take shelter while en route to somewhere else. If not that, then an expression of the paucity of existence for the anonymous majority. Helen had half-heartedly made it her own by tacking the cover of the surrealist magazine, The Minotaur, on the wall. It was a picture by Max Ernst of a robed and skeletal looking bull-headed man.

The bed was narrow and uncomfortable for two but they made do. Fabian awoke suddenly one night to see a man at its foot. He sat up in alarm. Helen was sleeping deeply and did not stir. The man was thin with close cropped blond hair. He sat for a while without moving or speaking. Fabian could see him because they had fallen asleep without turning off the bedside lamp. He was very pale, not just his hair but his skin. It was translucent, like the skin of an eft or salamander. He didn't appear to be threatening, but Fabian was nervous and he could feel his heart racing. Then the man turned slowly toward him.

"Don't worry. I'm not going to hurt you. Just lie down and go back to sleep."

Fabian did as instructed. The next day when they got up, he told Helen what had happened. She passed it off as a dream. She may well have been right but it certainly didn't feel like a dream. It stayed with him. The theme of an unexplained visitation was to later recur in his film, *The Theory of Five Thousand Footsteps* where a couple of gangsters wake up a man who is asleep with his wife. They hold him down in the bed, threatening violence unless he gives them something which they don't specify. What follows are a few agonising moments until they depart as mysteriously as they had arrived.

That morning they were up early and he decided to walk to work. It took him over an hour and a half. He was slowed by the previous night's calamities and by his bad leg. Fabian was still young enough not to see his injury as a debilitating problem. It was an annoyance that was bound to improve and wasn't worth thinking about. He was not someone to be hindered by adversity. His mind was occupied with the pale man. It would be easier to accept that it was all a dream as Helen had said, but as he walked, he imagined different explanations. At first he thought of the man as a benign being whose purpose was to look out for him—a guardian angel. But then the apparition could have been Helen's guardian angel and not his. He soon discarded that idea as too simplistic, puerile even. He re-played the scene to himself. The pale man had been sitting at the foot of the bed in profile, seemingly engaged by his own thoughts. He had sat that way for some time before turning to speak. The words he had spoken were dismissive, though not rude or angry. It was most likely that whatever this man was up to had nothing to do with him or Helen. They just happened to be in the same place. The door had been locked. In the morning Fabian checked the window—that had been locked too. So how he had managed to get in, and then out again, was a mystery. Maybe he had the key. Maybe he lived there. Fabian imagined a myriad of existences all wrapped up together, yet unconnected and separate from each other, except on the rare and inexplicable occasions when the barriers fell away. Someone else was living in Helen's room. Not very likely. So maybe it was a dream after all.

When he got to work he had the sense that people were avoiding him, not physically but with the flickering aversion of their eyes. He brushed it off, justifying his own anxiety by thinking that any one of these people could have lost someone during the night, or had received some bad news. They had to keep going but that was the grim reality for all of them.

This was to be a big day for Fabian, the first time he would be allowed to operate a camera on his own. He wasn't worried about it. He knew what he was doing. He realised that it had been six years since he decided he wanted to make films. Not that what he was about to do could be called a film. It was on film, and that was about the extent of it. He was going to be working on a public service announcement for the government, to discourage people from spreading rumours.

He had barely taken his coat off when he got word that Mr Beddington wanted to speak with him. He instantly knew that something was amiss.

"Take a seat, Davis."

Fabian lowered himself into an armchair. Jack Beddington stood before him, looking down. Fabian had a similar feeling to what he remembered from his schooldays when summoned for a beating. A feeling of powerlessness and formality. A feeling of inevitability, where nothing could be done but undergo the next moment. He knew what was coming.

There was an awkward silence. Mr Beddington paced around, visibly upset.

"I don't know how to say this, so I'm going to come right out with it."

He paused again, as if mustering himself.

"Your family home was hit by a bomb last night. I'm afraid you have lost both your parents. I'm very sorry."

Fabian felt as if the world around him was swelling. He could hear his own voice sounding distant and faint.

"I see."

"We thought you were there too. But fortunately, you were not."

Fabian had nothing to say. He was thinking of his parents. He had never been particularly close to them but they had been a staple of his existence, the only family he had. Now he had nothing. He hoped it had been quick.

Beddington was pacing again.

"I know it's not much of a consolation but it was a direct hit. They never would have known what had happened. Look Davis, I think it would be a good idea if you took the day off. Give yourself some time to come to terms with this. We'll pass the "rumour" job to someone else. Don't worry, there'll be other opportunities. Are there any family members you could talk with?"

"No. Just me. But if you don't mind, sir, I would prefer to keep working today. It's the best thing for me to do."

"Well, if you think you can manage it."

"One must live while one still can."

"Yes indeed. These are trying times. Very trying."

CHAPTER 9

FABIAN TOOK THE PICCADILLY line down to Ealing Common. He spent the train ride in a daze, wondering if the pale man was somehow connected to the death of his parents. By the time he had reached Ealing Studios,[1] where he was to work that day, he had decided that there was no link. It was coincidental, yet he still found himself doubting the randomness of coincidence.

His work went without a hitch. It was filmed on a stage set of a pub with a suspicious looking man telling a credulous blonde woman a scurrilous rumour. He wasn't completely happy with what he had done but no one had questioned his ability and, as the expression went— it was good enough for government work.

At that time the Ministry, or the government, was obsessed with rumour as damaging to morale and as a sinister enemy tactic. Later, when no evidence supported that view it was quietly dropped for the sake of better things. He had done his bit, and he was glad he

---

1. Ealing Studios is the oldest functional film facility in the world. It has been in continuous operation since 1902. It was repurposed for sound recording in 1931.

had not taken the day off. To mix with others, whether he liked them or not, tempered his reality. Had he been left to his own devices he would have succumbed to moroseness.

Afterwards he went over the road to the Red Lion and had a pint with the actress. He tried to get her to accompany him up the street to look at a bomb-site but she wouldn't have it. Instead he went to Staines and stood before the rubble that had been his home. The houses on either side of it had also been destroyed. It was hard to distinguish them. The violence was so indiscriminate and incidental. It was excruciatingly painful. He never went back there.

Fabian stayed at Helen's for a while until he found a place of his own. He rented a flat at 27 Conway Street in Fitzroy Square, not far from where he worked. It was a basement flat, dark and dingy, with an entrance by stairs from the street. He would often encounter a large rat on those stairs, which probably lived in the vaulted cellar below the pavement, among the dustbins.

He was soon to inherit a substantial amount of money. It took some time to make its way through the courts before it reached him. Fabian never thought much about money. He was aware of its necessity but didn't lust after accumulation for its own sake, or for the status it would provide. He was not a spendthrift or prodigal, he had little desire for material possessions. There was nothing he really wanted except to be able to pursue his own interests. He knew that would require money but just assumed it would be forthcoming, and forthcoming it was.

This is quite easily explained by Jupiter in the Eighth House, which enabled him to benefit financially from death without having to think about it. He gravitated towards a bohemian life, a trait that grew stronger as he got older. In that respect he was going in the opposite direction to most people. His life always remained a curious blend of solitude and gregarious extroversion. He liked other people but he preferred to be by himself. Despite that, Fabian was generous. He was later to provide funds for the education of Helen's daughter Phoebe. Beyond just giving money, he gave of himself. Phoebe recalls the excitement she felt whenever he came to visit: "he gave me his full attention. It was pure and focused." They would sword fight on the landing, and up and down the stairs. He would take her on long walks and talk to her about fabulous mythological creatures and exotic buildings hidden in impenetrable jungles. He would make her laugh, as when he impersonated a monopod on the street, with no regard for the opinions of people passing by. Fabian loved children, though he never had any himself, and could relate to them in a simple, unselfconscious way, never talking down to them and always brimming with fun and enthusiasm. "Father disapproved of him with a sort of awkward, begrudging tolerance."

The last months of 1940 were fraught with hellish fiery nights and imminent invasion. The Prime Minister promised victory some time in the future. How that was going to come about, was not explained. Still, there was hope.

By the end of the year, Fabian had made a friend. Charlie Bryce was a new employee at The Ministry. He had returned from Dunkirk without his right arm. Unfortunately he was right-handed. He had been both a talented painter and writer before his injury and was not going to allow his creative abilities to be stymied by the loss of an arm, so he hammered away incessantly on one of the Ministry's typewriters with his left hand, trying to retrain his brain. He said he had always wanted a typewriter and now he had one, even though it was not his.

Charlie was assigned to The Films Division. They joked together that between them, with Fabian's two arms and Charlie's two legs, they would make a complete man. Soon an easy closeness developed between them. Fabian was always able to get along with people but aside from Helen, he had never had any close friendships. Charlie had an absurdist sense of humour. He had a way of expressing things that spun new meanings to the most mundane of subjects. Nothing was out of bounds. He could find silliness in everything, even in the loss of his own arm. Yet it wasn't a humour of denigration. It had an underlying optimism. Fabian found that his experience working at the Ministry was transformed. He began to enjoy coming to work in a way that he hadn't before.

The second friend he made at the end of that year was not human. She was a Yorkshire terrier and he called her Gruff. It was the first name that came into his mind when he agreed to take her. She had been rescued from a damaged building and he instantly recognised in her face the need to give and receive love. He understood that animals suffered just as much as people did in wartime, something he had never thought about. So he took her back to Conway Street and she slept in the crook of his right arm, her snout nuzzled into his armpit. His mother had never allowed him to have a pet. She thought animals were dirty.

Chapter 10

1941 SAW AN INCREASED workload at the Ministry of Information. Fabian was called back before the army medical examiner and again failed his physical. Though perhaps Mr Beddington had pulled some strings. There was a constant flux of people coming from the war to the Ministry and then going back again. It was hard to maintain continuity and Fabian had become invaluable. After the death of his parents, Jack Beddington had taken a personal interest in him. He was never summoned by the army again and spent the rest of the war at the Ministry.

Fabian was now directing informational shorts. By coming up through the ranks, even at an advanced pace, he had built up enough practical knowledge to understand the job of each crew member. He did not try to control minutiae but he knew what he was asking of people and his demands were not unreasonable. He was very young to have reached that level. The products he made were extremely dry. It was hard for him to get excited about films that encouraged people to grow vegetables, or avoid wastage. He was always looking for ways to give them more pizazz. He used his newfound prestige with the boss to get Charlie on his writing team and they began a collaboration which was to last into the post war years. Though they were limited by their subject matter, Charlie brought a subtle absurdity to the government films, just as Fabian had hoped. They had a quiet conspiracy between them to introduce humour. It was not strident enough to become a problem but made the projects more interesting for them. They laughed together about the actor they had made converse with a cauliflower.

A theme that interested him was to describe the experience of an individual who had looked deeply into himself and discovered there was nothing there, and then lived with that knowledge. Perhaps this was akin to the alienation of existentialism, though not completely similar. Psychologically it might be understood as the worldview of someone who had not been loved enough. He liked to question the hierarchies of importance. He tried to portray this by keeping his subject and the relevant unrelated objects in the foreground and using a wide angled lens. In the government films he made about growing vegetables he surreptitiously tried to show that the shovel had the same importance as the person who used it.

Knowing that nothing lies at the heart of everything but that there is an illusion to maintain, forces all people to become actors. There was a dissociation between the actors and the lives they were acting, and that was what Fabian liked to explore. This underlying theme was not perhaps as bleak as it seems. In the disconnection there was room for humour, that strange, unquantifiable quality which enables one to shift realities and kill pain while expressing it—a way to sidestep suffering. In mediaeval times humour referred to vague metaphysical states within the body such as melancholy, or biliousness. It seems to have moved on from the medical science of the day into an even more abstracted realm. What would have caused it to do that? Had humanity started laughing at its errors?

If all things were of equal importance, then all living beings had an equal right to life. He was annoyed by hearing people refer to animals with possessive pronouns. To assume ownership of a dog, or any other animal was the epitome of anthropocentrism, which he regarded as ignorance and stupidity. He became a vegetarian.

Fabian experimented, when he was allowed to, with other techniques to develop his style. Aside from his frequent use of wide-angled and flat-field lenses, he tried out unorthodox camera angles, either too high or too low, often tilting the camera off level. He also played with sound by overdubbing the actors reciting their lines again after a scene had been shot. At first this was because he wasn't happy with the sound quality, but he discovered that it had an added reality-skewing, off kilter effect. The immediacy of the initial acting was affected by the re-enacted voices divorced from the visual and physical world. It had to be the voices of the actors who had originally played the parts. The voice of another person did not cause the same effect. Everyone belonged to their own voice, just as it belonged to them.

In 1942 Fabian worked on the film *Listen to Britain* in a subordinate role as an assistant to the director, Humphrey Jennings. He got the position due to the film's producer, Ian Dalrymple, who had taken a liking to him. At that time all the films and radio broadcasts produced by The Ministry of Information, along with their posters and signs, were propaganda. Jennings believed that the British people were averse to brazen propaganda, which they associated with totalitarian regimes. He therefore couched the message of the film in ambiguity, cutting back on the usual narrative voice, using music instead, creating an effect that came to be described as a kind of cinematic poetry. When he saw the finished film, Fabian was very impressed with this ambiguous quality. A message hidden in ambiguity might mean that viewers would be unaware of what they were receiving—they would have the space to create their own meaning from the structures presented to them.

Fabian left the Ministry in March of 1946, when it was dissolved. Although The Crown Film Unit was still in operation, he wanted to work independently and found himself gainfully unemployed. Around this time, his inheritance came in and he moved to a new flat in Manchester Square. Charlie Bryce was also unemployed and they spent many hours together talking about the films they wanted to make. It was a fecund time and they both became so close they could intuitively grasp each other's ideas almost without speaking. Out of this period came the film *The Theory of Five Thousand Footsteps*, which was released by The Rank Organisation in 1949. It was made on a shoestring and did not do well at the box office, partly because Rank didn't put any money into advertising it, and also because its subject matter was too far beyond the mainstream for popular appeal. In later years it received recognition and respect. It was shot with a minimal cast and crew mostly on London streets.

The idea had started with a short story that Charlie Bryce wrote and hand delivered to Fabian on a few sheets of paper, rolled up as a scroll. Together they adapted it to a screenplay. It followed the downward, or perhaps lateral trajectory of a man who crossed London on foot, from West to East and who ultimately disappeared on the Isle of Dogs.

Little did he know at the time that it was the only film he would ever make.

CHAPTER 11

The Theory of Five Thousand Footsteps
Story by Charles Bryce

John Eldritch woke up in the middle of the night to find himself pinned down in his bed, a knee on his chest and his arms grasped firmly below the elbows.

"Just tell us where it is and you won't get hurt."

There were two men in the room. He could see them in the moonlight, which spilled through the gap between the curtains. There was a full moon that night.

"Where is it?"

The knee pressed down on him with greater force. He felt disorientated, the dream he had been roused from slipped away and became a sensation of pain. The two men were not part of his dream. They were in his bedroom. He knew he had to say something.

"I don't know what you mean."

Elizabeth was awake, lying next to him, silent with fear. She wasn't being held down. Suddenly she sat up.

"Leave us alone. We don't have what you want. You've come to the wrong place."

The other man who had been standing by the bed roughly pushed her back down.

"Shut up and lie down."

Then the one with the knee in his chest spoke again.

"You better tell us where it is. You're running out of time."

The second man was searching the room, rummaging through the chest of drawers, pulling books from the shelf and tossing them to the floor, shaking them first to see if anything was hidden between the pages.

Then with a sudden click of the door they were gone.

Elizabeth got up from the bed and turned on the light.

"My God, what a mess."

She began to pick up the books and close the open drawers.

"What did they want? We should call the police."

John was still lying down, relieved that the intruders had gone. But they'd be back. He'd have to find a way to throw them off.

"No. I don't think we need to involve the police. They obviously had the wrong address. No harm done."

"But what's going on?"

"I have no idea."

But he did. They had not been given the wrong address. He knew what they were after. The irony was that it was right there in plain sight if they had only known where and how to look, though that kind of observation was an acquired skill. It had taken him since childhood to master it—from sensibility to knowledge.

Those gangsters were probably in the pay of some unscrupulous wealthy person—an American millionaire most likely, one of those rank egotists who hoped to leap-frog off his efforts and beat him to the prize, employing all the best equipment that money could buy.

They had come looking for his plans, his maps, his notes—but he was not foolish enough to keep anything like that lying around. He had known for years that secrecy was paramount. He hadn't even told Elizabeth. He trusted her implicitly, though there was always the possibility she might gab. Besides, if she knew what he hoped to discover and exactly how he intended to do it, she might think him mad as a hatter and their marriage would no longer be as secure as it seemed.

He wondered about his sanity sometimes but was reassured, because if he was capable of wondering about it he must be sane. It was all part of the life he had chosen for himself, one of the many trials an explorer must face when setting out into the unknown, with only his passion and conviction, and a deep loneliness to accompany him.

That questioning of his sanity gave him an idea. If even he wondered about it, then it shouldn't be too difficult to convince others. His opponents and competitors would soon lose interest and leave him alone if they believed him to be utterly mad.

With that in mind he paraded up and down Saville Row one Saturday afternoon in July, wearing a pair of snowshoes. He spent some time loitering in front of the building that had once housed The Royal Geographical Society.

He chose that street for its potent symbolism. Gone now were the days of those great luminaries Burton, Speke and Stanley who had been his childhood heroes. He could imagine their voices echoing off the walls and he could also imagine himself there too, presenting his case to the members of the society. They would probably have laughed him out of the building, heaping vitriol upon ridicule, for his claim to have discovered a place that they would have considered impossible to discover. A city that had stood for so long could never have been discovered, only built, and then expanded upon ever since. His claim was ridiculous.

In his opinion, the heyday of the Society had been the Victorian era—a time when learned men were confident that they understood the framework of knowledge. If there were gaps, they could be filled, hence the trips into the dark continent. They were innocents really, just not pure and unsullied like young children. In this case their innocence was tinged with arrogance—not two words commonly associated, but apt nonetheless. After all, in their day Western science had only coalesced from alchemy, astrology and hermeticism just a hundred years previously. But time had changed the content of minds. That self-assured framework had crumbled and rotted, leaving a ruin that seemed strangely anachronistic with a powerful emotive residue like a lone Victorian folly on a desolate landscape.

He loped up and down the street all afternoon until he was moved on by a policeman and was forced to go home, leaving the ghosts of the orgulous gentlemen of the Royal Geographical Society to talk amongst themselves for eternity.

They didn't have to talk that long, as he was so satisfied with his performance that he went back the next day. This time, along with the snow shoes he took a cabbage which he held in one hand at arm's length from his face and spoke to incessantly. It was harder than he had imagined to keep up a constant stream of gibberish so he resorted to reciting passages in Latin from memory—passages from Julius Caesar's Bellum Gallicum and the occasional poem by Ovid.

Odi concubitus, qui non utrumque resolvunt. Hoc est, cur pueri tangar amore minus.[1]

Things had seemed to be going so well—until he was arrested, charged and later convicted for causing a public nuisance, and fined a small amount. His plan had perhaps been too effective. He was employed as a bank teller at Lloyd's but lost his job when the bank manager found out about his conviction. He was deemed unsuitable to be in the position of handling money. After that his life began to devolve. Funds were tight. A bank teller's salary had not provided him much opportunity to save and the small amount he had disappeared quickly. When that was gone the house went too, and soon after that so did Elizabeth. He didn't have family or friends who could help him, so in a relatively short time he went

---

1. "I don't like intercourse that doesn't make both lovers come. That's why I'm less into the love of boys." From *Ars Amatoria* by Ovid.

from a stolid lower middle class existence, in a mock Tudor house, to the streets.

It was a meteoric descent that would have shaken most people but John Eldritch had a confidence which was founded on an image he had of himself—that of a man with a deep sense of purpose, strong as a horse and keen as mustard, a man bound to succeed through sheer determination and courage alone. His misfortunes were lessons from which he could learn. His life had been a dress rehearsal for this expedition. He taught himself to grow stronger in adversity. He could not foresee all the difficulties he would face but he knew there would be many, and tried to prepare himself as best he could. He urinated on his shoes to soften the leather, because he knew he would walk great distances. The loss of his wife, his house and his job helped him to slough off the impediments to his vocation. He would now be able to set out sooner than he had previously thought, and this prospect made him cheerful.

He set forth in the early morning when most people were still asleep. He was going to discover the City of London, he knew it was there.

He was no fool. He was aware that London was a functional modern city that had existed in some form since the Roman times, or even before. That could not be denied. His customary reticence was not only due to his fear of being outflanked by more powerful and unscrupulous operators but also because most people could simply not understand his ideas and would consider him odd, derailed or insane. If he was successful in what he aimed to do, he would deserve a place in history. The impact of his discovery would ripple across the fields of knowledge. It would be a point from which there was no turning back, like the European discovery of the Americas. It would forever change the world. He just had to find it—the London inside London—the lost city. This was no archaeological expedition. He was not looking backward but around him, for this city was lost in the present, not the past.

Years earlier an idea had occurred to him, which he called The Theory of Five Thousand Footsteps. It was more an intuition than an idea, a way of noticing the invisibles—the people who had walked on the streets of a city, and those who were yet to walk there. Surely these people had buildings to enter. They were invisible too. Invisible but present. He was certain of it, and just had to train himself by forging a new connection between retina and brain for them to appear.

He had read a lot in order to give substance to that intuition and over the years it had become an idea. Quantum theory, although he could not claim to understand it, seemed to give it possibility. He also read about biology and optics. If light was to bend around an object, then it would render that object invisible to most eyes.

The neurobiological mechanics of sight, along with the broadly similar mental equipment of most people gave credence to the assumption that the external world was clearly defined, cut and dried. Any object outside one's body could be seen and felt. From this coordinated trickery of the senses was born a basic certitude. It was suckled and maintained by a body of knowledge that people no longer needed to think about and could just take for granted. It was a bit like money in that regard, where the exchange of tokens became a purpose in itself, and the original symbolism was lost to irrelevance.

His theory could have applied to anywhere in the world but he chose London because he was familiar with it and because of the light there, which he attributed to its latitudinal position. The light especially on a sunny day had a particular quality that could best be described emotionally—a beautiful, forlorn clarity.

He was heading East from Acton, copying the cardinal direction taken by Sir Richard Francis Burton when he walked across Africa from West to East, and who, it is said, was cured of syphilis from the high fever he suffered along the way. The advantage of discovering London was that its latitudinal position meant that the lines of longitude were closer together for him than for Burton in Africa, as they bulged further apart nearer the Equator. This was an example of how measurement influenced experience, and he presumed that it would facilitate his discoveries.

By mid-morning John Eldritch stood before St Paul's, gazing up in wonder. It was the same feeling of awe and surprise that Cortés and his men must have felt when they had first looked upon Tenochtitlan. Some of that shock might have been due to the sudden realisation that there were other people in existence who could build such a city. He had a similar feeling. It was said that St Paul's had been designed by Christopher Wren. He stood there a long time saying "Saint Paul's, Saint Paul's, Saint Paul's..." over and over, until the words lost all their associations and meaning. It was a technique he used to unfocus his mind and prepare it for discovery. But there was to be no discovery that day. He noted down the details in his journal.

"Dome undulating. The smell of wasps but no breakthrough."

He had the habit of falsifying his location in his journal. It was an attempt to throw off the millionaire and his thuggish henchmen. They might have supposed he was spending the night in Marylebone, when in fact he was in Shoreditch. The stakes were too high for him to be upstaged. History would be misinformed. It was an unfortunate necessity.

He had good intentions for his journal. Aside from listing his progress and discoveries, he wanted to write a detailed report about the sexual customs of the natives. His journal and a knobkerrie were all he had brought with him. The book he carried in a canvas bag, belted to his waist, and the staff he leant upon, or swung as he strode. It could also be used as a weapon should the need arise. It had been useful when he fought off some aggressive geese in Kensington Palace Gardens.

The days passed. Many of them. He dispensed with dates in his journal and only used the names of days. So far he had found nothing. The tabulation of dates with numbers was the kind of calibration that kept him in the world he was trying to leave, and he blamed it for his lack of success. The use of names alone was much less constricting. Names could be followed to different places.

At some point he began to use the same day for each entry.

"Wednesday. I have found nothing today. I catch glimpses that confirm my hopes but that is all."

"Wednesday. Woden. Do I know him? Have I met him?"

"Wednesday. I believe I have found a native who might help me."

That native went by the name of Mary Elder. She came upon him on Whitechapel Road. For some reason, perhaps due to his degenerating physical condition, he broke his own rules and told her that he was searching for the London inside London, and the London inside that. A long, looping list. "The strange thing is…"

he told her, "all the cities that contain other cities are themselves contained within others." It was as if the inside and the outside were the same thing, and that thing was not one but many. It was such a radical truth that it would change the way life was perceived. All he had to do was find it, and he was close. She listened to him talk without disagreeing or interrupting. It was obvious to him that she had knowledge about these matters, maybe even more than he had, so when she suggested that he accompany her and that she would get him something to eat and take him to a place where he could wash and sleep safely for the night, he went with her meekly. It was only natural that she did not divulge her knowledge. She was protecting it just as he would. On the way to wherever they were going she asked him a number of times if he drank. Each time he replied that he did not. He didn't drink, he didn't smoke. He kept himself in fine fettle. He was also a vegetarian but he didn't tell her that. These questions about drinking had to be a sign, if he could only work out its meaning. He suspected that it must have something to do with the sea, or a river and he decided that when he had cleaned up and had some refreshments, he should probably make his way over to the Thames.

How many times had she asked him if he drank? Was it three times? Three times he had denied it. There must be some significance to that. The clues were presenting themselves to him on their own. Mary wanted to know if he was a veteran. Yes, as far as he knew he had been in North Africa with the 8th Army. They had obviously arrived at their destination. It looked like a social club. A door open to the street revealed a large room with tables and chairs and a few natives shuffling around inside. They were all male. Outside the door another native stood ringing a bell.

This intrigued him. He pulled his journal from the bag and quickly scrawled into it:

"Wednesday—The sound of a small bell."

He soon came to the conclusion that this man, who Mary Elder referred to as Mr. Simpson, was narcoleptic. He rang his bell constantly to keep himself awake. He looked as if he was about to keel over but he was still able to insist that the knobkerrie remain outside.

This was an annoyance but there was too much to lose, so he decided to acquiesce and left it leaning against the building. The big room inside smelled of stewed meat and disinfectant. In conjunction with the tobacco smoke it made breathing an unpleasant necessity. He had the sense that he was closing in. This was some interstitial place. He was not expecting to walk through a door into one of the other Londons. That would be too convenient. It was an idea familiar to most people, probably because of the symbolism of doors. The reality was much more complicated. It had more to do with probability and perception. He had always admired science and what appeared to him its epistemological qualities but the objectivity it championed, though a powerful analytical tool, had always seemed flawed to him. It sidelined subjectivity and relegated it to a state of frivolity or human imperfection. But to remove subjectivity was to take the experimenter out of the experiment. One day perhaps it would be possible to conduct experiments with machines, but then the machines would merely be substitutes for the humans they had superseded. In that case they would be subjective machines. There was no getting away from it—objectivity and subjectivity could not be separated. They had to be taken together.

It was this uniting of opposites that gave him the blurred clarity he needed to find what he was looking for.

Mary Elder led him in. She was the only woman in the place, as far as he could tell. He had to learn more.

"Are there any particular sexual customs in this area?"

"Come along now Mr Eldritch."

"My observations have led me to believe that there is a higher frequency of homosexuality in the West End than anywhere else in the city but I wonder if I am wrong."

"Just go through that door. You can wash and get some clean clothes. There's a gentleman who will help you. Then come back here and have something to eat."

She was avoiding his enquiries. She must be protecting something. And she knew his name.

He went through the door and then through another, to find himself in a bathroom with four shower stalls and a line of benches stretching along the opposite wall. There was a sink at the end of the room. No sooner had he entered than an old man came in, wearing a stiff jacket and peaked cap. He was missing some teeth. He held a towel.

"Well who do we 'ave 'ere then? The Prince of Wales? Take off your clothes mate, and wash off the filth."

They stood looking at each other. The old man showed no inclination to leave.

"Well go on then. Don't be shy. I was like you once, back from Ladysmith, broken, fond of a tipple and nowhere to go, till I came 'ere."

"And you have been here ever since?"

"That I 'ave. But enough of this glorious persiflage, governor. Strip down. The serpent sheds 'is skin and throws it in that basket over there, see?"

When he realised he would get nothing more from this beady-eyed man he took off his clothes and stepped into the shower.

The water felt good, not hot but lukewarm. There was a bar of soap, well worn with brown stains that looked like rust and he lathered it up. He couldn't recall the last time he had washed.

"Come on then. We don't 'ave all day."

He turned off the water and stepped out of the shower, reaching for the proffered towel. As he dried himself the old man dragged a bench over to the sink.

"Sit down 'ere and we'll give you a shave."

For a man so old, his hands were adroit and he didn't leave a single nick. When he was finished he left the room to put away the shaving things and came back holding a suit on a hanger with a shirt and some undergarments.

"Put these on. They're about your size."

The clothes were threadbare but clean. They looked twenty years old. The suit was a little too large but he cinched the waist and cuffed the ankles. The old man stood back and looked up at him with feigned astonishment.

"My old aunt! Aren't we the fancy man. When's the wedding? Now off with you. Run along up front and get yourself some comestibles. There's a good lad."

Back in the main room he took his place at the food table. Mary Elder appeared to have left. When his turn came to be served, he declined the stew and asked just for boiled cabbage. The native with the ladle made no move to fill his bowl and simply stared at him.

"It is customary to give thanks."

This was unusual. From where he came it was customary to give thanks after receiving something and not before. If the man would fill his bowl he would thank him. It was merely a matter of a second or two, but that small increment of time seemed to have undue importance in this place. He wondered if he had passed into the version of the city he had expended so much time and effort to find, without having noticed. It was natural enough, he supposed, with multiple places that occupied the same space—the boundaries were not apparent.

He held out his bowl.

"Thank you very much."

"That won't do."

"I'm sorry. I'm confused. I thought I just gave thanks."

"You must thank your maker and apologise for having led a life of sin."

"But I haven't led a sinful life."

"We are all sinners. If you are too proud to admit it and refuse to abase yourself, then leave now. You are not welcome."

John Eldritch looked around. He was outnumbered and the knobkerrie was outside. It would be best to move on, while he still could. He hastily tied on the canvas bag, which he had retrieved before the old man dispensed with it, and made his retreat. The bell ringer was still tinkling. His stick was where he had left it.

As he walked out into the street he felt a delicious disorientation. No food but no matter. Despite his hasty departure, he knew that he was finally reaching his goal. He just had to get further in, and then apply that sturdy objectivity so respected by science. And then he would have succeeded. The Royal Geographical Society be damned.

All night he followed the course of the Thames. He was in no hurry, pausing frequently for extended periods to take in the effect of his surroundings. The sound of the footsteps from his urine-soaked shoes hitting the pavement in a rhythm both steady and imperfect, made him acutely aware of himself and then freed him from that knowledge. The river was wet. That he knew. But who could say what wetness was.

This metaphor would find the solution, itself a metaphor—homogeneous dispersion.

By dawn he had reached The Isle of Dogs. His confidence had grown, commensurate with the rising sun.

"Wednesday. The Island of Dogs. The dogs have all dissolved. Ambiguity is the baseline of information."

This was his last entry. The journal was found by Kevin Smith, a schoolboy at George Green's school. Kevin gave it to his father, who was not particularly interested and left the book outside. Rain soon began to erase the words.

Time and mildew did for the rest.

Chapter 12

After *The Theory of Five Thousand Footsteps* had flopped, The Rank Organisation wanted nothing further to do with Fabian. He had used his connections with industry professionals at The Ministry to get it made. They had put in a good word for him and talked up the film's value but now even their enthusiasm seemed to wane. It left him feeling lonely and depressed.

When Charlie had first given him the story he had immediately recognised its strength and appreciated the way it was sensitive to his own ideas. Together they had turned it into a script and had enjoyed the little details like having John Eldritch talk to a cabbage.

Fabian had felt a growing excitement as funding was approved and the idea came closer to reality. They cast Bradley Meadowes as John Eldritch. He was a stage actor just beginning to cross over into films, and was perfectly suited for the part. Ginger haired and wiry, he looked just like an intrepid explorer, and he had a dark side too. Fabian was able to handle his frequent bouts of drunkenness and turn them to good effect.

He spent months planning every shot and finding locations. The film was a joyful obsession, and all through the process of making it he had felt as if he was stepping forward on the path of a glittering career.

Then, after all that effort, it had fizzled out in an anticlimax worse than anything he could have imagined. It was a heavy blow but he was not about to give up. Despite rejection, he knew he had talent. He just needed to crawl away somewhere and rethink his approach.

Though he was not short of money, he did the unexpected and took a job in a warehouse on the Great West Road, near the Hoover factory. He wanted to get as far away from the film business as possible for a while. He spent his days wheeling a pallet around and loading it with tinned goods. Day after day, pallet after pallet. It was hard on his knee and most of the time he was in pain.

At 10 o'clock every morning there was a tea break. The workers gathered in the break room and a woman called Maureen would come in with a tea trolley. They'd sit around drinking their tea, looking at the newspapers. One man was a voluminous talker with an encyclopaedic knowledge of football. He could remember every team, every match, every goal—from years back. Another one had been in the Navy, most of the time in the brig for going AWOL. He said the meals in there were main course and desert, all on one plate, mixed up together. He had tried to get out of the Navy by pleading insanity. He definitely had some problems with spatial judgement as he would quite frequently roll his loaded pallet off the edge of the dock in the loading bay. Then there was the man who was able to urinate while walking, without ever getting a drop on his clothes—a strangely impressive feat. Fabian, with his public school accent, didn't really fit in with them but they tolerated him and mocked him gently.

He lasted there a month. On his final day a shard of glass fell suddenly from the skylight above. He could feel the air it displaced as it whistled past his cheek and embedded itself into a tin on his pallet. It had the shape of an isosceles triangle. Had its path deviated by an inch it would have buried itself in his skull.

Never again did he work a day job.

He spent his evenings reading, with Gruff curled up beside him. He was ensconced in *The History of The Conquest of Mexico* by W.H. Prescott. He knew there was a film in it. He was not interested in making an epic. That would be an obvious choice, seeing how the story was so remarkable and sweeping in scope but that approach would best be left to Hollywood. It would be difficult to raise the money it would take. His idea was to not try to portray the whole event, as if viewed from the outside, but to go inside it, through the eyes of one individual. La Malinche was a possible contender—a real person and a legend—slave, traitor, victim and symbolic mother of a new country. The fact that she was an interpreter was all the more important. Perhaps without her Cortés would not have been successful. Before she learnt Spanish she could not translate directly and there had to be another interpreter present. She would translate from Nahuatl to various Mayan languages, which would then be translated into Spanish by another person. This three-way interpretation allowed for the possibilities of mistranslation, which Fabian knew he could exploit to deepen the mystery. He felt strongly attracted to her, even though they were separated by nearly five centuries.

Alternatively he could look through the eyes of a soldier and adventurer—a penniless young man dreaming of an *encomienda* that would never be granted. Someone like that would leap at the chance to make his fortune with Cortés.

Perhaps this man would be taken prisoner and somehow avoid being sacrificed. Fabian could see the Aztec priests, their hair matted with blood, one of them wearing the skin of a man who had just been flayed.

He wondered how so few men had been able to bring down such a vast and powerful empire. They'd had help of course. They certainly were not lacking in bravery, but they seemed small minded and barbaric from a modern viewpoint. These were men who gave each other women. La Malinche had been given to one man as a reward for his deeds but then Cortés had taken her when he discovered her abilities as a translator. Then he gave her to someone else, after she had borne his son. Was religion the cause of their small-mindedness, or was it the other way around?

Before he had finished reading the book, he had decided that he should go to Mexico and get a sense of the place and its history. Then he would return with brimming notebooks and he and Charlie would put a film together. He was sure Helen would look after Gruff while he was away.

CHAPTER 13

ON OCTOBER 3RD, 1952, the day that Britain carried out its first atomic bomb test, Fabian boarded The Queen Mary at Southampton.

He had decided to go to New York first and then take a train across the country to El Paso, from where he'd enter Mexico. He had never been to America before and was excited about the trip. He had bought a Cabin Class ticket, which meant that he would not be travelling in luxury but he would not be completely denied it either.

After they had left Cherbourg, and headed out to sea, the vast expanse of water began to unnerve him. Meals were a distraction and so he had made a foray into the dining room that first evening, half hoping to meet someone and embark on an onboard romance, but knowing that dining was a distraction only lessened its distractive qualities and he spent most of the first day and a half in his cabin. He had a porthole but all it revealed was greyness. He was becoming listless and lay back on his berth.

He had been thinking a lot about the film he planned to make. The conquest of Mexico was a big subject and should readily lend itself to the cinema but he couldn't find a way in. He wasn't about to make a historical drama—any of that sort of thing would be peripheral. He would explore the significance of the event with the character of one person, through whom he would pass into the subterranean, mythical turbulence of it all. He wanted the audience to feel an emotional impact which could not be explained. The problem was he had no idea how to do it, and the character he sought eluded him no matter how hard he thought. It was as if his imagination had become as grey as the sky.

Perhaps the bleakness outside had the latent quality of a blank sheet of paper and there were so many possibilities that he didn't know where to start. He could always hand the whole thing over to Charlie, who never seemed to have any trouble coming up with things but whose ideas were sometimes flippant, and Fabian worried that Charlie might not be able to appreciate the depth of the film, which he didn't understand himself yet. No. He would have to formulate the idea first and then hand it over. After that Charlie could tart it up in his usual fashion. Then again this film might just be a pipe dream, something shallow with delusions of profundity, in which case he was wasting his time.

He got off the bed and went up on deck to get some fresh air. The weather wasn't good and there were few other passengers about. He leaned over the rail and stared down. It had always amazed him how the Vikings traversed oceans in open boats. His eyes followed the side of the ship down to the water. He looked at all the painted rivets and the rust that rimmed their edges. The sea-spray felt clammy on his face.

"See anything interesting down there?"

Fabian was taken by surprise. He had been so involved in his own thoughts that he hadn't expected conversation. A woman in Wellingtons strode confidently towards him. She looked him up and down. For once in his life he couldn't think of anything to say.

"I'm…I'm not sure."

By now she was beside him at the railing.

"You must have been born in January."

These were odd words from a stranger but he couldn't help liking her for them. She had guessed his month of birth. It was unlikely though not impossible—one chance out of twelve.

"Yes, that's true. I was born in January. How did you know?"

"I didn't know. I just surmised."

They both gazed down at the swell.

"What would lead you to surmise something like that?"

"My profession."

She looked about ten years older than him, although he was never a good judge of a person's age, especially not a woman's.

"What is it you do? Are you a psychoanalyst?

"I'm an astrologer."

"A professional astrologer?"

"Yes"

Fabian imagined a branch of the civil service filled with astrologers, taking the train each day, giving celestial advice about dairy farming, or the prisons, or the miners, or the... suddenly he was hit with an idea.

"You draw up horoscopes and interpret them?

"I do."

He could get her to cast a chart for the character he was seeking. It was the perfect solution to his problem. It was better than perfect. It would be a completely new approach to writing or film making. The creator would have no knowledge of his characters. It wouldn't be creation in the literal sense but more like meeting strangers, people with their own futures. The surrealists might have intended something like that with their automatism.

"Would you be interested in casting a horoscope for me?"

"I'm going to be busy in New York with a conference...but perhaps after that."

"No. It would have to be sooner. I'll be travelling. Could you do it while on board and have it ready before we dock?"

"Maybe. Though I won't have time to interpret it."

"And what would you charge for something like that?"

"Thirty guineas."

It was an outrageous amount. He could live off that for three or four weeks.

"That's a bit steep don't you think?"

"Well, do you want the horoscope?

He had the money. He had brought a veritable war chest with him, locked away in his cabin. He didn't know exactly where his travels would take him, or for how long. He had come prepared.

"All right then but you must guarantee I have it before we leave the ship in New York."

"I'll need payment first."

This was not the onboard romance he had imagined, but no less intriguing. Even the ridiculous fee excited him.

"We'll meet at dinner and I'll pay you then."

She had a pad and pen in her hands that he hadn't noticed her pull out.

"Very well. What is your date and place of birth? And the time if you have it. If not, we'll call it noon."

Fabian did some quick calculations. If his character was a young man accompanying Cortés on the Mexican invasion, he would likely have been born between 1490 and 1500. As far as he could remember, many of the conquistadors came from the Extremadura region of Spain. He wracked his brain trying to think of a town in that area. Mérida. That sounded familiar. He would use his own birthday. Why not? He just had to think up a time of birth.

"That would be the 20th of January, 1494 in the town of Mérida, Spain. The time of birth was 5:47 am."

She raised an eyebrow as she wrote down the information.

"You're much older than I thought."

He grinned. "You thought it was for me?"

"It usually is. Now the date.... Is that the Julian or Gregorian calendar?"

He had not taken this into consideration. It didn't matter to him as accuracy was not a concern but he didn't want to divulge his motive. He never liked to talk about his ideas before they were fully formed.

"I think you have me there."

"The Gregorian calendar replaced the Julian after a papal bull in the 1580s."

"I know what they are, I just don't know how it applies in this case."

"Then I suggest the Gregorian calendar. Does this individual have a name?"

"Fabián.... Fabián Dominguez."

"An ancestor?"

"Not exactly."

"You know the time of birth for someone who lived almost five hundred years ago? Is this a real person?"

Fabian turned on his charm, locking his startling eyes to hers.

"Thirty guineas should preclude such questions, don't you think?"

"Are you a veteran? Were you wounded?"

"No.... Why?"

"That knee of yours.... You should look after your knees."

A few hours later he handed over the money and a package was delivered to his cabin by a steward before the ship docked.

Fabian had no knowledge of New York. He took a room at the Hotel Chelsea, which Dylan Thomas had recommended. He spent the first few days ensconced there with Fabián Dominguez' horoscope, and venturing out down Sixth Avenue. As he walked alone in this unfamiliar city his mind was filled with the adventures of his namesake in New Spain.

Chapter 14

"By the fingernails of Christ!"

That's where things took a turn for the worse. The man opposite him suddenly stood up from the table, knocking over the bench behind him. He was a big man and his ugly face was wracked with a spasm of fury. He spluttered his oath and Fabián felt the spittle on his cheeks and lips.

Up until then they had been having a friendly conversation. Though strangers, they shared the same disappointments. They had both come to Trinidad dreaming of opportunity. But here favours were only dispensed to friends or kinsmen of the Governor. There would be no *encomienda,* no matter how much they thought it was their due. There was a bond of dissatisfaction between them, and their mutual complaints were a comfort to them both.

The big man had lurched outside to piss, and then returned to his seat, broodingly silent. His mood seemed much changed. Fabián, drunk himself, put it down to the bad wine.

Then suddenly there was the sound of the falling bench, clattering against the flagstones as the man sprang to his feet.

"By the fingernails of Christ!"

Fabián could make no sense of it. The man was yelling at him. He seemed to think that he had been insulted.

Fabián could not remember exactly what he had said but he was sure there had been no insult. He imagined his father shouting at him. He was a profligate wastrel, a stain on the honour of his family. No good would ever come of him. He stumbled to his feet and somehow managed to get outside. The big man came crashing through the door behind him.

He clasped a knife. Short and evil, it protruded from his clenched fist. Even with his reason marred by wine, Fabián knew there was no escape and that he should move in close to hamper the man's mobility. Before he had time to plunge his knife, Fabián drove his fist up under the big man's nose with all the force he could muster. He was shocked by the copious amount of blood.

The next day he awoke anxious and with an underlying sense of gloom. No matter how far he had come, he still seemed to be in the same place. Then he remembered with a jolt the proceedings of the night before. Had he killed a man? Would he soon be arrested? They had been seen together in the tavern.

Waiting for the unknown became unbearable and he decided to go into the town and see if he could learn anything. Perhaps if his worst fears were confirmed he would flee into the countryside.

He passed by the tavern and there was no corpse on the ground. That was a good sign. But then if there had been a body, it would probably have been removed by now, so he could not afford to be complacent.

When he reached the port he discovered that ten ships had arrived. Most of the people in the town had flocked to greet them. The Captain General Hernan Cortés was leading an expedition and he was looking for able-bodied men.

When he heard this Fabián decided he must sign on. It was a moment like glancing at a woman and instantly knowing that she was the one he would marry. Everything fell into place despite his headache and unsettled stomach. It would be an escape from potential legal trouble and from unrequited hope. He might even enrich himself, and he would no doubt be doing something more interesting than working on a farm.

"Name?"

"Fabián Dominguez."

"Where are you from?"

"From Mérida in Spain, sir."

He was standing at a table, set up on the quay and the quartermaster, who was recruiting, sat with quill in hand.

"How old are you?"

"Twenty-four."

"Are you married?"

"No"

"Next of kin?"

Scratch, scratch, scratch went the quill. His eyes wandered off to the swaying of the masts as the ships bobbed at anchor. God, he wished he had a horse. Things would be so much better.

"Next of kin?"

The quartermaster had a bulbous nose—a drinker's nose.

"None. None here that is."

The scratching quill paused as if it doubted him somehow.

"Do you have any experience, boy?"

"At sailing a vessel, sir?"

"At soldiering."

"I was with Juan de Grijalva last year."

That seemed to clinch it, even though it was a lie.

"Do you have a horse?"

"No, sir"

"What weapons do you own?"

"A crossbow. And a sword."

"Are you proficient with the bow?"

"I am, sir."

"Very well. You are signed on. You will get your share of the proceeds after the King's sixth and the Captain General and officers have taken theirs. Put your signature or mark here."

He thrust the quill at Fabián and reached into a purse at his side, pulling out a single coin.

"Report back here in a week. Don't be tardy. The Captain General is keen to set sail. Bring your weapons and some provisions. What food can you bring?"

Fabián clenched his fingers around the coin in his palm. "Cassava bread and some salt pork, sir."

"Come back here a week from today, ready to board by sunset. Your ship will be the San Sebastien."

Chapter 15

The fact was, Fabián was not as adept with the crossbow as he had claimed. Beyond winning it at cards he had no other experience with it.

That became apparent when they were put to target practice on the island of Cozumel, where they sojourned before crossing over to the mainland.

On his first shot he missed the target completely. Then he felt a sudden blow to the back of his neck, which brought water to his eyes.

"Call yourself a crossbow man?"

His assailant was Pedro de Guzman, who along with Juan Benitez was in charge. It was their duty to make sure the crossbows were in good order and to whip the men into shape.

Guzman looked at him with a quizzical expression and underlying scorn.

"Your life and mine depend upon you being able to hit a target."

His life was full of half truths and grimy suppositions. He was lucky he had reached the New World before they had instituted the licence system, otherwise they never would have let him come. And he had come—but for what? To waste his time on someone else's farm? To witness the death of hope? It was a succession of moments, of whorehouses and wagers, of spilled wine and dreamed opportunities.

Now he finally had a real opportunity and he couldn't even hit the target. He glanced around him at the others. They never seemed to miss. He was a counterfeit.

As so often happened when he sank into despair and self-loathing, he found himself clutching at them for comfort, as on a cold night a man might huddle in his cloak, seeking some fleeting warmth. When he realised that he was looking for solace in his own misfortune, then the great weight that bore down upon him instantly withdrew, leaving him light headed and euphoric. Then his melancholy turned to confidence. It was always this way. He was protected by saints, who had the habit of arriving at the last moment.

His companions might shoot their bolts and laugh at his ineptitude but he could dance around them with words.

He had a way with words and a voice that people found pleasant. A mellifluous voice delivered from a face that was handsome, but not too handsome. Not handsome enough to provoke resentment. Not handsome enough to hold up a mirror to those imperfections that were the lot of so many. But handsome enough nonetheless. He knew his strengths and he knew it was time to answer Guzman, who was still talking.

"What kind of a man are you anyway?"

Thoughts were timeless and barely a moment had passed since he had been punched in the neck. And what a blow! Guzman was a rugged professional soldier and not someone inclined to sympathy. Fabián could see the hairs that extended from his nostrils like the bristles of a boar and the expression in his eyes pondered violence. This was the brink. Any self-justification would be foolish.

"Well, obviously not a good marksman."

The violence in Guzman's eyes became a grin.

"Hah...a soldier who cannot fight. A bird that cannot fly. If you were a painter you'd be blind. Pull yourself together, lad."

And he moved on.

After that, Guzman made a point of teaching him to shoot and how to maintain his weapon so that it wouldn't let him down. By the time they left Cozumel in March, Fabián had improved and considered himself just as able as the next man to kill people with a crossbow.

His improvement led to more daydreams about the wealth and position that awaited him across the water.

The Indians in Cozumel were friendly and helpful but they displayed a certain reticence in accepting the true religion. They said they had been worshipping their own gods since time immemorial and saw no reason to change. Captain General Cortés was persuasive. He instructed the carpenters to build a cross and an altar to the Virgin, telling them that if they showed due respect and attention to its care, they should never want for food and the Virgin would protect them. Usually Cortés was very concerned about keeping on good terms with the natives and made rules about how they should be treated. Infractions were punished harshly. But in this case, he sent some men to destroy their idols, as an added act of persuasion and because he held God and the Virgin in such high esteem.

There was no resistance, just a crowd of silent onlookers. They went into the priest houses, which were usually situated on platforms, and threw the idols down. Fabián thought they were the most disgusting abominations he had ever seen. In one room he entered, behind a curtain, was an idol clothed in human skin. There was also a priest who was in the act of slicing his own member with a stone knife. They threw them both off the platform.

These sights lingered in Fabián's mind. He discussed it with his companions. There was no room for error in this venture of theirs. The future did not seem so assured.

One morning, a boat made from a hollowed tree arrived on the shore from the mainland, not even four leagues distant....

***

FABIAN WAS INTERRUPTED FROM his thoughts about the conquest when someone took the seat opposite him. For hours he had been looking out of the window at the landscape as it sped past him. There was not time enough to take in the beauty before it became something else and he had been lulled into a state where he forgot about the view. Then a woman had sat down opposite him and he had turned his face from the window to glance at her. She calmly returned his stare without saying anything and made no attempt to acknowledge him. Fabian found this odd. Acknowledgement was the way strangers assured each other they meant no harm. It seemed a very basic behaviour. She sat straight with her bag on her lap and showed no sign of being troubled by his gaze. Aside from her bag, which was small and elegant, she had no other luggage. Their close proximity and her impenetrable demeanour made Fabian feel tense. Conversation was out of the question. He wanted to study her face but he found it impossible and turned back to the window.

He reached for his book on astrology, making use of the opportunity to cast a surreptitious glance. She was still in the same position, looking directly at him. He opened the book and read a few pages but could not absorb the information, so he leaned back and shut his eyes. Soon the gentle clatter and lurching of the train made him doze.

When he opened his eyes he saw the woman had gone. Perhaps she was in the dining car, or the lavatory. Then he noticed that she had left her bag on the seat. Why would she do that? It was small and white, made from a creamy leather, with a gold rim and clasp at the top—what he gathered the Americans called a pocket book. Why would they describe a handbag as a book? Was it because it was small enough to fit in a pocket? But then women's clothes tended not to have pockets as far as he could tell. Perhaps it was a euphemism to avoid some obscure embarrassment about needing to carry items around—feminine items that were considered taboo.

He wondered what might be in the bag. A compact, keys, some money—something that would identify her perhaps. As much as he would have liked to satisfy his curiosity, he knew it would be wrong to rifle through the bag. It would be an invasion of her privacy and privacy was something he valued. So he let it sit there, tantalising in its stillness. After a few moments, and with some guilt, he reached over and raised it to his nose. There was a trace of perfume. The leather was soft and of high quality. He probed it with his fingertips. There was something hard inside. Then he put it back on the seat, with slight embarrassment as if someone might have noticed him smelling a woman's bag. He looked around but there was no one who could have seen. The woman would no doubt come back to retrieve it when she realised it was missing.

The hours passed but she never came back. The bag on the seat had a great significance for something so small. Why did she have no other luggage? Perhaps she did, and it was stowed away in the baggage car. When she reached her destination one of those porters in the red hats would help her with it, rolling it on a cart to a waiting taxi that would whisk her off to a five star hotel.

As he had nothing else to go on, he used his imagination to speculate on who she was. Somehow his musings on Soviet agents, illicit romance and wealthy fugitives were unconvincing. He was unable to picture her—he couldn't even remember her hair colour. He realised he had no idea what clothes she was wearing. This was unusual for him. He had keen powers of observation. There was nothing for it but to put his reservations aside and look in the bag. He glanced around to make sure he was not being watched and reached across for it.

Inside was a box. He carefully pulled it out and peered into the bag. There was nothing else. He set the bag aside and held the box to his nose. It had that same faint perfume. When he raised the lid he saw a small book and an iridescent bird feather. The book looked very old—brittle parchment bound in cracked leather, a wizened rectangle only about four inches by three. Scrawled across the pages in faded ink, and in a fine hand, was a nonsensical jumble of letters, not in any language he could recognise. It had to be a code of some sort. He closed it carefully and slipped it into his pocket. Then he closed the box, leaving the feather inside, and put it back in the bag, which he replaced on the opposite seat just as he had found it. He glanced up and down the carriage. Nobody could have seen him.

Chapter 16

I was staring out over the parapet, a beautiful view of the reservoir before me which I did not appreciate. I was consumed by my thoughts.

This story I've been telling of Fabián the conquistador is dull. A contrivance. When I first struck on the idea of using an astrological chart to define him, as with the other Fabian, I was pleased with its recursiveness. Recursion gets to the heart of existence. It is a light constantly reflected between two mirrors—but a fraction is lost in each journey until in the end there is darkness. Just as there was in the beginning, as some people believe. I'm not sure there was a beginning.

This astrological jaunt was a conscious effort on my part to be no more than a steward, or the cog in some antiquated machine that spewed out fiction. In such a process my personality, or style of writing would be irrelevant. In that way I would be freed from myself, only limited by a set of calculations that did not involve me. Whatever was produced would be a byproduct of sidereal reality.

But once I had decided on a second chart, I never finished interpreting it. Instead I delved into the *Conquest of New Spain* by Bernal Diaz. I had persuaded myself that some kind of research was necessary and that might have been the problem—why I was now gummed up in a dry tale. Another problem was how to tell an interesting story when the principal character doesn't understand the language being spoken around him.

Obviously I would need to pick up the chart again, or have the other Fabian do it. He was no doubt checking into a hotel in Mexico City. He would have time.

The horoscope was exciting enough but with some chagrin I wondered if it meant giving up the idea of Fabián being imprisoned in a pyramid. I had wanted to explore the Aztec concept of thirteen heavens—though heavens might not be the right word, being too associated with the Judaeo-Christian tradition. The word 'levels' didn't do it justice either. What could it be? Zones, domains, layers? Layers of reality, or irreality?

A man who is lost in thought is an unpredictable thing. A roller skater, barreling along, limbs flailing for increased momentum, should know that. He should react in advance to avoid collision. I didn't see the skater as I turned from the parapet, the image of Fabián waking on an earthen floor still occupying my mind. Then we saw each other and both dodged in the same direction. And then in the other direction. And then the collision.

I fell and hit my head on the road. Had I been wearing a helmet, I might have avoided the concussion I suffered, but then pedestrians don't usually wear helmets.

***

Quilted armour, though better than nothing, did not provide much protection against their swords—wooden sticks inlaid with sharpened stone, as sharp as steel. Fabián had seen a horse decapitated with a single blow.

He raised himself and felt his aching head. So much for his helmet. There was dried blood in his hair. He must have been hit by one of the stones that had showered down upon them, along with the spears and arrows. The heathens would have dragged him unconscious to this place. He had no memory of how he had arrived. And what of the others? Had they been able to get away?

He was lucky he had not been killed outright, though he knew it was just because he was to be killed later in one of their demonic sacrifices—a worse fate than to die on a battlefield.

There would be no escape unless God chose to intervene. It did not seem promising. He would do best to direct his entreaties to Maria. As the Mother of God she might still love a wayward son, no matter how vile his transgressions. He mumbled his prayers of contrition, trying to picture her, as she gazed down tenderly at the infant in her arms. Instead he saw a man with hair that hung down to his ankles, shaking a brazier and speaking a torrent of unintelligible words.

This priest was soon joined by three others, equally hirsute, reeking of a slaughterhouse, tinged with the resin they were burning. They were talking in turn, as if in liturgy. Then they bound his wrists and led him out to the street.

Fabián squinted around him. He was forsaken. There would be no help from the Virgin. He knew then that the man he had left on the ground outside the tavern had died from his wounds. He was to be punished for murder. This hell would be replaced by another, for eternity.

The streets were busy. The people had returned and stared at him as he passed. He thought he noticed a hint of awe in their eyes, before they looked away. It was hard to tell. He was flanked by two priests. An older one walked in front and another followed behind. Fabián noticed that the priest ahead of him, who seemed the most senior, had a stumbling gait, which slowed their progress through the streets. He had seen this gait before, in some of the men at the camp in Cozumel. A number of them had to be relieved of duty for a few days and had been sent back to the ships to lie on the decks. Though by the time they had set out to the mainland, they had all recovered from this mysterious affliction. It was no doubt due to the bad air of the place, or perhaps the water.

He mumbled his prayers as he followed the swaying priest. Ave Maria. Again and again. The rhythm of the words lulled him and carried him. They seemed to give the world a brilliance. He could remember the empty streets of yesterday, which seemed long ago now. The town had been devoid of people then, but not of those strange birds native to this land. The men had abandoned their formation with mirth and gleeful shouts as they chased the fowl up and down the streets. Supplies had been scarce at the camp, as the Indians who would bring them food had mysteriously stopped coming. They snatched up whatever they could from the empty dwellings.

When they left the town a few hours later, an army was waiting for them in the fields. Ten thousand faces painted black and white, wave upon wave, stood in silence. Suddenly with a great roar, they attacked.

Their opponents were massed so closely that each shot from the crossbows and arquebuses met a mark. The Indians were surprised at so many casualties and fell back. Soon they regrouped and came on again. This cycle of onslaught and withdrawal continued until they managed to get close enough for their arrows and javelins to have effect. Soon after that they were fighting with swords.

The battle seemed so distant now.

Chapter 17

"I was ten years old. It hadn't rained for a long time. Then it did. I sat under a tree with my back against the wall. The rain was heavy but it didn't last long. When it was over I watched the water drip from the leaves. I stayed quite still. A childhood of poverty left no time for thought beyond the struggle for survival—how to steal a crust of bread or avoid a beating. That was usually its extent. But as I sat there with nothing much to do and the water swelled on the leaf points and fell to the ground, it occurred to me that there had to be something more. Then I understood that a great amount could be created by small, almost unnoticeable things. That's when I started stealing with intent, beyond the commonplace thieving I did for food. Drop by drop, drip by drip I stole, year after year until I had amassed enough to raise myself and gain some respectability."

Fabián would never have known this man was Spanish. He looked like one of the townspeople. His hair was shorn like theirs. He wore nothing but a loin cloth.

They were walking together away from the town. Fabián could not understand why this stranger was telling him details of his childhood. It was as if he was confessing a crime. The words were an inescapable torrent. His head was throbbing. He felt dizzy and sick.

It was when the people around him had started falling to the ground and lying listlessly, with flies buzzing about their eyes, that the man had approached him.

"*Estás muerto,*" he had said with a gravelly voice, as if he was no longer familiar with his own tongue.

Fabián was shocked to hear Spanish again. It had seemed so long since he had been able to understand what was being said to him.

"What happened with the battle? Did they get away?"

"Barely, but they got away."

Instinctively he did not trust this man, whose name he later discovered was Guillermo, but he needed his help. He knew that in his condition he would probably not last the day without him.

"What do you mean I am death?"

"You were to be given to Xipe Totec, a god of death, regeneration and plague. The victim must impersonate the god. That's why you've been dressed the way you are."

"It's disgusting. It's a religion of cannibals."

"We eat the flesh of our own God and drink his blood, don't we? A God who was sacrificed."

"That's different."

Guillermo was quick to point out that there was no great difference between the ritual execution of prisoners, and burning people at the stake after first breaking them on the rack, as was the custom in Spain.

To make such an equivalence was tantamount to treason. Fabián found himself wondering about this man's town of birth. It could not be Mérida. No one from there would talk like that.

"As you were a soldier taken in battle you were to die in combat. Do you see that rock over there? It's a sacred stone. You would have been given a sword with a blade of feathers and then tied to that stone, where after some symbolic resistance you would be killed by a warrior. Then your heart would be cut from your chest and the skin flayed from your body. By impersonating the god you become him."

Fabián's skin crawled at the sound of those words. After the old priest had died, the others had taken him to a temple and made him dress in these strange clothes. He looked down at the red sandals on his feet. Those priests—they were all dead now. It had been hard to tell with their grime and their satanic language, but he sensed that after he had dispensed with his Castilian clothes they had regarded him with a kind of deference. Though that hadn't prevented them from knocking him around. But his prayers had been answered. Having no jailers, he was able to escape from the room in their temple and come down the steps into the town. People had fled in terror.

"They got more than they bargained for when they took you prisoner. You've come down from your twelfth heaven to walk among them. You have been chosen."

Fabián's mind was reeling. These last few days had been a whirlwind.

"They have twelve heavens?"

"Thirteen, actually."

"Why so many?"

"Why not?"

"How is it that you know so much about these people?"

"I have lived among them."

"You have forsaken the true God."

"I have forsaken nothing. To live among is to become, as the wafer on your tongue at mass becomes flesh."

Fabián didn't like this conversation. It was dangerously heretical.

The town was empty again. Anyone left alive had fled. No one remained but the dead. Guillermo was looking into the houses as they walked along the street.

"We need to find food. It will take us three or four weeks to reach Tenochtitlan."

Fabián could make no sense of what was happening. He had been in the midst of a battle. He had miraculously escaped sacrifice and now he was stumbling along behind this evil man in a deserted town. Everything was disjointed. He was exhausted and wanted to lie down in the dust before he fell over. Then, as he staggered with fatigue, his eyes were filled with a burning light, so bright that it blinded him. He could feel the divine will surge through him, energising him. After a moment the light faded and he could see again. Suddenly he understood. As an incarnation of this heathen demon he was to be the instrument, the weapon even, that would clear this land of idolaters and sodomites. He had become more powerful than armies. Already, people had died at his approach. He was the flayed man, the scourge of God. Yet still he felt frail in his invincibility. He did not know if he had strength enough for the task. He could sense the frivolity of his previous existence. This was how it must feel to be chosen. Whatever fear he had experienced before was nothing compared to now.

If he had been chosen by God to be His vengeance, why was this man still alive? He was an apostate. He should be dead, yet he looked remarkably healthy and vigorous. It could only mean that he was part of the divine plan and had been chosen to act as a guide. It was a relief to have direction again. This was obviously what God intended. He should go to Tenochtitlan.

The days were hot, his feet were blistered. He had discarded his red sandals along the way. As the days passed, Fabián no longer felt pain and fatigue. Each step took him further and further from the person he had been. He ceased to notice his surroundings. He was lost in his thoughts, which no longer made sense to him and over which he had no control, as if they were the thoughts of God and he was merely their vessel.

"Your captain, Cortés, is a mediocre man...."

Guillermo was conversing with someone. He seemed to expect a response, but Fabián didn't hear an answer. Guillermo kept talking.

"I knew him in Cuba. He doesn't seem to have any talent beyond a certain low cunning."

Fabián's body was not his own. He had become a part of God and existed only as disease. It had come into this world from the twelfth heaven. There were thirteen heavens and thirteen people present at The Last Supper.

"Cortés has accomplished nothing. He has no skill as a commander. In fact he is barely in command at all. Governor Velasquez chose him precisely because he is a mediocrity. Someone more capable might thwart his own ambitions."

He could hear Guillermo in the distance talking about how the great Motecuzoma had a large complex of buildings adjacent to his palace that housed a collection of wild beasts and that three hundred people worked there.

"He not only collects animals—jaguars and a wide variety of snakes, lizards and birds, but people too. He is interested in the ungainly and deformed, the dwarves and giants. Oddities. He wants some Castilians in his collection. Your captain thinks he is engaged in a glorious act of conquest. He does not understand that he is being deliberately led to the heart of the empire. He is going to end up in that collection, along with his men. As will you my friend, if you and Xipe Totec don't kill everybody first, of course."

Chapter 18

Fabian had returned from Mexico depressed. He had expected to discover an idea—a strange new interpretation of cataclysmic history, but had come back with nothing. Maybe there was no such idea. The ruins he had visited were interesting but silent. Even the mysterious ball courts did not speak to him.

Over a few months, his lack of inspiration had festered. Everything he had previously attempted now seemed futile.

He had visited Helen in Oxford, bringing as a gift a pre-Columbian figurine he had found in a field. They discussed his problem. Talking about it only made it worse. It gave reality to something that otherwise might have remained just a possibility.

He left with the name of a psychoanalyst in London—Dr Paul French. Helen had problems of her own.

***

"You need to find the courage not to create."

Dr French sat back in his chair and gazed at the wall. Fabian was uneasy. The few therapy sessions he'd undergone with this doctor had not resulted in any transformations or higher awareness as far as he could tell. He was likely being too impatient.

"I'm not sure I quite understand what you mean."

"A distant mother, a rigid authoritarian father. Both parents emotionally unavailable. A lonely childhood. You would need solace. The idea of film-making provided you with that sense of purpose and confidence denied you by your parents. But you see you're coming at it from the wrong direction."

"But what do you mean by the courage not to create?"

"Now that you seem to have lost your creative drive, you are desperate to get it back. You cling to the idea because without it you are forced to confront yourself. You are afraid. That's not such a bad thing. Fear will be your guide. In fact your writer's block, or whatever you want to call it, means that the process of integration is already underway. For you creativity is a crutch. To alleviate your limp you must discard it. It has become an obligation—a hindrance. So you need to develop the courage not to create, to take the risk of letting it go. Ignore the sirens who sweetly tell you otherwise. If you wish to be creative, you must cease wishing to be creative. Of course, it's not as simple as that."

Dr French was unorthodox, seemingly not in thrall to Freud like so many of his peers. He didn't hold back from expressing an opinion yet he never revealed himself. The only nihilist analyst in London, Fabian speculated with sardonic amusement. That amusing thought sparked an interest that countered his antipathy. Though Dr French seemed bored, he was never slow to respond with a cutting observation. His fee was unorthodox too.

Fabian wondered what benefit Helen got from talking to him. It made him feel as if he didn't know her.

He was wary of spewing out his private thoughts to a complete stranger whose interest seemed cynical, so he withheld things. He took care not to mention his relationship with Helen. He didn't talk about the ghostly apparition at his bed many years before, or the strange multicoloured bird in the sky above the beach at Durdle Door—all of which seemed significant in an obscure way. Selective revelation was perhaps counterproductive, from what he knew about psychoanalysis but Dr French had a glibness that did not inspire trust. When he talked about 'alleviating the limp', he showed no empathy or understanding of the problem Fabian faced with his knee. He would never walk without a limp no matter how integrated his psyche.

"You know, something that bothers me is that I sit here talking about myself but I know nothing of you. It doesn't foster trust. Why would I divulge personal details to a stranger? Especially as I'm someone who values my privacy."

"Why would you indeed? Though people do generally like to talk about themselves. But my personal life is irrelevant—to you at least. For you I am a mirror."

"So if I look at you I see myself?"

"Yes, but you might not recognise the person you see there. He might be one of the selves you have repressed, or one that is latent."

"Going back to what you said about the courage not to create. It strikes me as missing something. Would you say that to Leonardo da Vinci?"

"I am not talking to Leonardo da Vinci. I am talking to you." He paused and appeared to be looking down at his notes. He seemed irritated. "I think from now on it would be beneficial to limit our sessions to seven minutes."

Fabian wasn't sure if he was being serious. His smug delivery might be humour, or he might be trying to generate a reaction for some unknown reason. Or maybe he was just responding with anger to criticism.

"Seven minutes seems remarkably short."

"It does. That is exactly the point. It will make us focus on essentials."

"I imagine your fee would be reduced accordingly?"

"No. It won't change. If you are uncomfortable with that, I could offer you three and a half minutes for the same price."

Fabian understood that he was making an allusion to the story of the Cumean Sybil who showed up in Ancient Rome and offered nine books of prophecy to King Tarquinius. When he baulked at the price, she burnt three and asked the same amount for the remaining six. He baulked again and she burnt three more. He eventually bought the last three books for the price she had originally asked for nine.

Fabian suspected that this sudden reference was a distraction. Dr French was finding a way not to speak about himself.

"Are you saying that from now on our appointments are to last only seven minutes?"

"No. It was merely a suggestion. It's up to you."

It was a radical idea to compress therapy sessions into such a short time. Fabian wondered if the same compression could be applied to the feature film, and a couple of hours could be reduced to just a few minutes. Would there be a loss of depth and detail? The information would have to be packaged to fit into a small temporal space. Changing the way a story was told would change the story itself. He glimpsed prospects on the horizon.

His glimmer of hope soon faded. Audiences would never trade their cinematic expectations for a sudden burst of information. It would be economically unviable to fill cinemas for only a few minutes. Where would people hold hands and caress each other in the dark if there were no cinemas? The same stories would be told, in the same way, in the same places. There would be no revelatory flashes of light. He would be forced to follow some lumbering script.

"I feel somehow as if my life is preordained."

"Are you talking about a sense of fate?"

"No. Not fate or destiny. Not God or religion. Nothing like that. It's more the sense that I have to conform to a script by a writer who is not particularly talented, and who didn't so much write the script as interpret, or translate some other text. Does that make any sense to you?"

Fabian thought he detected a flicker of interest from the doctor but it might just have been the motion of his eyes as he focused them on the clock.

"That's all we have time for today. Shall we say the same time next week?"

He was writing on two different notepads simultaneously, which Fabian found strangely disturbing. "Give some thought to those seven minutes I mentioned."

***

Later, Fabian telephoned Helen. He was curious what she thought about Dr French.

"He seems cynical and bored. Not qualities one would look for in a doctor, don't you think?"

"I get your point, Fabian, but appearances aren't the final arbiter are they? I think he has an unusual kind of wisdom."

"What kind of wisdom? He only looks about fifty."

"Wisdom isn't necessarily equated with age. You know that. Don't be so facile. And anyway I suspect he is much older than he seems."

"What makes you think that?"

"I don't know. It's a hunch"

"Helen?"

"Yes..."

"Do you want to get married?"

"Oh fuck off."

Chapter 19

Dr French was tired. It was not just physical fatigue but mental and emotional—tired from wandering and carrying the burden of secrecy. He was the loneliest of men. It hadn't always been that way. In his youth, at the age of ninety-seven, he'd had the stamina of a twenty-year-old mortal. Numerous people would have attested to that, had they been alive. There was only one who still lived. She was the one he had cursed with the gift of his knowledge. At the time he had thought he was helping her. It had not seemed a curse but a blessing, earned with painstaking labour.

How he longed for Juanita. He had no idea where she was. He had last seen her in Tenochtitlan. That was over four hundred years ago. It was Mexico City now. They had drained the lake and filled it. Was she still there?

What had first seemed the promise of eternal life revealed itself as a relentless task to adapt to changing mores, languages and science. The only thing that had remained constant over the ages was inexorable human folly, a perpetual unraveling that even the purest knowledge was impotent to stem. The new-fangled bomb that could destroy entire cities was a profound misunderstanding of Nature, masquerading as a perverse form of progress.

The problem with endless adaptation was that as he gained new knowledge he could not forget the old. He was a wineskin perpetually filled to the point of bursting, but forever denied the relief that final rupture would bring.

If only he had Juanita and his book. He imagined she must be lonely too. How could she not be? Together they would relieve their loneliness. With the book, he would find a way to work backwards and reclaim mortality for both of them.

It contained his formulae, written in cypher—a most ingenious invention he had taken years to perfect. He doubted anyone could break it. He still remembered the key, as clear as daylight. He just had to find the book. Perhaps it no longer existed but he had to assume it did. There was nothing else to hope for. His one advantage was an inordinate amount of time, which would increase his likelihood of success, even if it took millennia. There was a chance that scholars had copied it, tempted and intrigued by his unsolvable code. He had been searching libraries and museums for hundreds of years. Those institutions had been improving and his prospects were not impossible.

Immortality did not preclude pain or imprisonment. The Alvarado brothers had not been able to endure being part of Motecuzoma's collection for long. They had needed very little provocation for violence. They believed they had killed him.

When he had known his arrest was imminent and not wanting the Alvarados to get their hands on his book, he had entrusted it to Fabián. He remembered how he had spun him that yarn when they first had met, how he had portrayed himself as a poverty stricken urchin who had robbed and stolen his way to respectability. He had lied for the sake of expediency, and a little for his own amusement. All that nonsense about the water drops had been a background to the story to give it the credence of a memory. Nothing could be further from the truth. The Emperor had desired a Castilian specimen before Cortés reached him and Fabián had been so gullible, so easy to convince he was an instrument of God. He had believed he was the bearer of disease, which he was of course in the opinion of the twentieth century. It was a strange coincidence that he now had a client with the same name. Unsettling. This new one might perhaps be a slightly more mature version of the old. Intelligent but still a fool. All mortals were fools.

His job as a psychoanalyst suited him. He did not have to speak so much as listen. His past could remain unknown. He never had to justify himself as the profession endowed its practitioners with a lofty impunity. He had been familiar with psychoanalysis since its inception, though it had been called something different at the time. He had dined with William James and been an occasional participant in the Thursday Club. He was well versed in the theory. Its language came easily to him and he could understand its origin, though the hours he now spent listening to people's inconsequential problems were an assault on his patience. It was his capacity to adapt that had made it possible for him to talk like a modern man. He didn't think like one. Everywhere these days was a trite, mundane obsession with individuality, while science had veered away from the arcane, embarrassed to be associated with alchemy. Knowledge had become partitioned. Ironically perhaps that was just as well.

After bribing his way out of an Ottoman prison, he had settled in England, an island so full of melancholy and bile. At first he had made forays to other lands. In Prague he had met John Dee and they became friends. They returned to England together and he spent many months as his guest in Mortlake. Dr Dee, who signed his letters to the Queen with the number 007 (a symbolic representation of being Her Majesty's eyes) had the most wonderful library. They spent many hours in conversation there. Dee was a brilliant man, though not as advanced in the Art as he was himself. A fact that had to remain secret. He taught Dee the way to measure the distance between two cities that he had learned in Baghdad, and Dee spoke to him of astrology and cartography and the movement of angels. He also discussed his idea of the great British Empire he envisioned for the future, something which had seemed unlikely then.

The library, as extensive as it was, did not contain his book, or a copy. He had searched it many times. Years later it was ransacked and burned to the ground, a devastating loss. By then they had parted company, due to a problem with Dee's young wife, and were not to meet again.

Along with the ubiquitous chaos and violence of the world related to the affairs of men, there now seemed to be a growing constriction. The means of transportation had much improved, and it was easier to move from country to country, but there had been a concomitant advance in the intelligence services of nations, as they were now called. He was expected to have a passport, if he was to cross borders. It was not such a simple thing to prove citizenship when he had lived so long, in so many different places. The overarching bureaucracy now required birth certificates, marriage certificates and so on. Things which were quite meaningless in his case. He would need the services of criminals to get around them. He might perhaps have hobnobbed with aristocrats and people of power to sidestep these new requirements but that would mean posing as an impostor like his old friend the Comte de St Germain. He preferred anonymity.

Money was not an object for him. He could make as much gold as he wanted. But these days gold raised difficult questions and he had to resort to criminals again to capitalise on it. Working for meaningless paper currency was simpler and allowed him a lower profile. Besides the transmutation of base metals into gold now seemed tawdry.

His visit to England had lasted much longer than expected. Dee's prophetic idea of empire had come to pass, and was itself passing as empires tend to do, hastened perhaps by two wars. He no longer desired to learn new things, or to travel. All he craved now was death.

He had of course survived a bombing in the most recent conflict and had been pulled from the rubble, shocking his rescuers by running off when they tried to load him into an ambulance.

Now he lived in a comfortable flat in Primrose Hill and worked as a psychoanalyst.

Would it never end?

Chapter 20

The English translation of *Foucault's Pendulum* by Umberto Eco was published in 1989. I read it and loved it. Many people seemed to think that Eco was using his extensive knowledge of mediaeval history, semiotics and philosophy to hoodwink or confound the reader as a kind of cheap trick and maybe just to capitalise on his success with *The Name of the Rose*. I thought such criticism was unjustified. The book was after all a satire about conspiracy theories. I read it again years later and didn't like it as much but still thought the original criticism was unwarranted.

I was very taken with the character Agliè, who may have claimed to be the Comte de St Germain, who himself had claimed to be five hundred years old. Both these characters, fictional and real, were most likely impostors and yet in the book there is an element of ambiguity that allows the possibility that Agliè really is the Count and he actually is five hundred years old.

I was so impressed with this idea that for a while I went around telling people I was seven hundred years old and was disappointed that everyone thought I was joking. There was no place for ambiguity in their lives.

I assume for no apparent reason that Dr Paul French was born in 12th century Al-Andalus when it was ruled by the Almohads, probably in or around Granada.

It seems to me that Dr French was not an impostor, though I suppose he might have been. Fraud can take on many guises. There could be such a thing as unconscious fraud, or a particular kind of fraud that pertains to fictional people.

Is a fictional character automatically an impostor by acting as real in relation to its text, outside of which it has no reality at all? What of a fictional character which pretends to be another fictional character? Do any of these entities bear any moral blame for their falsehoods, seeing as they were created by someone else? But then, everyone is created by someone else.

Eco formulated the idea of the open text—it has a different slew of meanings for each individual reader and for each time it is read. He might have drawn from the essay *The Death of the Author* by Roland Barthes, which radically questions the traditional concept of authorship.

I have tried in my own way to play with these ideas by using, or pretending to use, astrology to define characters and their trajectories.

Does any of this matter?

And who decides what matters or not?

I imagine that as human opinion is so fractured, the arbiter might be some shared common creation such as the free market. This I like to envision as a large network of warehouses brimming with manufactured products, from hardware to perishable items to intellectual property. Anyone can go there and take whatever they want, free of charge. That is obviously why it is known as the free market.

Chapter 21

So much had passed it almost seemed like nothing. Memories became dreams, and dreams faded away. Her life had become an endless experience of the present. She preferred it that way.

Juanita checked into a hotel. Behind the reception counter were two men, both dressed in white shirts and grey jackets with embroidered designs on their cuffs. It was most likely not the first time she had stayed in this hotel. They seemed to think they knew her.

There were clusters of comfortable armchairs, and glass-topped tables. On the walls hung sconces of semi-opaque glass, bracketed in steel. They provided a warm ambient light in the corridor where the guests who were disinclined to use the stairs awaited the lift. The doors to the street kept swinging open as bell boys wheeled in stacked luggage carts.

She stood by the main desk, slightly off to the side, waiting for the eager young man who was now retrieving her luggage from the taxi that had brought her from the station. There he was now—not using a cart—a suitcase in each hand, and her periwinkle blue hat box tucked under his left arm.

Her room was on the second floor. She would take the stairs. She preferred not to use the lift with its close confines, mute expectations and polished brass—all under the grim eye of the operator, his facial expression no doubt the result of spending each day going up and down and rarely breathing fresh air. Only those with the strongest mental constitutions could do such work. The rest went mad.

When she reached her room—number 21, the bell boy was already there. She folded the newspaper she had taken from the lobby and retrieved her key.

The door swung open. The bell boy held back, letting her enter first. She went immediately to the window and looked at the courtyard below. Luscious bougainvilleas tumbled from giant pots. Then she gazed at the bed cover—it was a creamy off-white with a slightly embossed geometric design, suggesting understated comfort.

The bell boy paused a moment after setting down her luggage. She turned and handed him a large banknote. If he was surprised, he showed no sign and just took it, putting it in the pocket of his waistcoat as if it were a coin.

She had often heard that it was a mistake to be over generous with servants. Such acts of profligacy only led these people to expect more. They were already indolent and duplicitous. Further encouragement was foolhardy. This was a mean-spirited idea to justify debasement. It reminded her of how her people had been enslaved. Money meant nothing to her.

She suddenly felt a sense of loss and couldn't decide if it concerned a misplaced object or something more abstruse. Then she remembered it was Guillermo's book. If she had lost it deliberately, then it had been an act of liberation. She had been carrying it around for centuries for no other reason than that she thought Guillermo would have wanted her to. She was tired of a life spent reacting to others, and from now on would follow her own caprice.

Her memories, like her lovers, were as numerous as the population of a medium sized city. That great number was a weight. Better to forget. Wilful, conscious forgetfulness brought peace of mind while leaving the possibility of remembrance intact. It was not easy to navigate an endless life.

She set one of her suitcases on the bed—the large green one with the leather straps, and started to unpack, putting her clothes in the drawers, or hanging them in the wardrobe. She slid her hatbox onto the top shelf. She was glad that she travelled with less luggage these days. When she had gone to New York she'd had big trunks with her, which she had filled with money, not at that time being familiar with banks. As the times changed, so did the luggage she supposed. Those years in New York had changed her too. She was feeling more detached again after her brief flurry with mortals. She had come here to see Tenochtitlan once more. Soon she would go to Europe, the birthplace of the conquerors. She would fly there in one of their aeroplanes.

When she was completely satisfied that all her things were neatly stowed, she went back down to the lobby. She helped herself to *The News*, which appeared to be an English newspaper, and perhaps for that reason caught her eye. If she was going to go there, she might as well see what they liked to talk about. On the front page was a story about a train crash that had killed one hundred and twelve mortals. She tucked it under her arm and then took a copy of *Novedades de Mexico*. As an afterthought she turned back and pulled an *Excelsior* from the rack and headed over to a vacant armchair. The lobby was crowded and in her haste to reach the one empty chair, the Excelsior slipped from her hand. She bent to retrieve it but another hand reached it first. She straightened up and was greeted with a smile. Disturbingly beautiful blue eyes stared for a moment into her own. They had the purity of a cloudless sky made more brilliant by a head of jet black hair. He handed her back the paper with a gentle nod and she watched as he limped away. The armchair was no longer empty. She returned to her room. The news didn't particularly interest her anyway.

CHAPTER 22

Charlie and Fabian sat across the table from each other at the Grafton Arms, a pub not far from his new flat in Manchester Square. It was the first time they had met since his return from Mexico.

"Double tops!"

An exuberant cry rang out from the alcove near them, where a game of darts was underway. Fabian looked over as a burly man removed the dart from the double twenty at the top of the board and disappeared from view with a swagger.

"It's a strange game, don't you think? *Fléchettes* in French—little arrows. Miniature archery or javelin throwing. A game of projectiles. There's something mediaeval about it."

Fabian had always been curious about games played in public houses, and how games themselves imitated life with their peculiar forms of analogy.

There was an awkward silence between them. They had shared so much but were now poised at that interstitial moment of reacquaintance.

"How was it in Mexico?"

All he could really think about was the book he had stolen. Perhaps he was meant to steal it. Or had she left it there on purpose, inviting him to take it? He could remember her sitting in the train, but could not picture her face. She must have been the same woman he had met in the hotel in Mexico City, when he picked up her newspaper. He wasn't certain though. He was usually good at recalling faces but he had been dozing in the train and hers might just be one of those faces that evaded recognition.

Whether theft or gift, it was a mystery that had upstaged his film. The book must have been five hundred years old. He had turned its brittle pages, its faded script almost illegible in some places, and had a strong feeling that this could be the idea he was looking for, even if it was unexpected and different from what he had supposed. He just needed to understand what was written. There was an attraction to something that could not be understood.

He had taken Dr French up on the seven minute therapy sessions and had come to look forward to them. He would often leave with a heightened sense of reality. If he looked at a tree he could see the veins in the leaves. The scent of flowers was more intense.

Fabian had expected they would talk about the subconscious but Dr French barely mentioned it and when he did he seemed annoyed, as if it was some shallow misconception. Contrary to the common assumption that consciousness resided in the brain, or was a side effect of its function, he inferred that it existed outside the self. That seemed an odd opinion.

The pleasant effects of heightened perception did little to allay his growing unease. It was possible that psychoanalysis was making him worse. He was a skein of contradictions but his opinion of such things had been changed by the unusual book he had just read—*Unnoticed Secrets*[1]. Opposites and contradictions no longer seemed so negative. He would accept them. To deny them would be futile. He would seek wisdom from a charlatan. That was why he kept going back even though he knew he was being fleeced. Perhaps he would tell Dr French about the book and would get an insight into its significance.

"It was interesting. But I didn't find what I was looking for."

Fabian glanced at Charlie's empty sleeve and felt a wave of sadness.

"Maybe you were trying too hard."

"Maybe."

He told him about the astrologer he had met on the boat to America and how the idea had come to him to get her to cast a horoscope for the principal character in his film, to whom he gave his own name. He had struggled to interpret the chart but had been distracted by Bernal Diaz.

"All I have are fleeting visions—a second or third grade conquistador, a bit of a wastrel on the tail end of feudalism. Thinks he's been chosen by God to spread disease. Red Aztec sandals on blistered feet. A Svengali like compatriot who leads him on a long

---

1. *Unnoticed Secrets* by Renata Scaduto, translated by Elliot Speare, Faber and Faber 1950. See Appendix 2.

walk to Tenochtitlan, for some obscure reason of his own. Perhaps he is working for Motecuzoma. And that's it. So full of gaps, it's almost as if this character I conjured with astrology, so that he would have some independence, has become too independent. He seems to have a life of his own and I'm not privy to it. What little information I have, I'm getting second hand. That's the way it feels. So you see there's nothing really there. I've come back uninspired. I think I'll shelve the project."

Charlie sipped his beer. "Well, as I said, I think you've been trying too hard. You need to relax and change your approach."

"How? In what way?"

"Use comedy. Don't take yourself so seriously. And maybe you should change the location. Forget about Mexico for the moment. What if your namesake is a down and out Englishman, in the Depression era? He meets a mysterious Irishwoman. They end up in a pub in Dublin. The landlord could be your Montezuma character...."

"Motecuzoma."

"If you say so.... The landlord could be called Seamus O' something. It would be perfect. They could all get drunk and have a glorious bar fight. Peter Sellers—the chap from The Goon Show, could play Fabián and maybe Montezuma as well. He's a fantastic comic actor and mimic. He's good at slapstick too."

"Why Ireland?"

"There's a natural parallel, don't you think? The colonial conquest of Mexico and, you know...the English in Ireland. But Fabian, you've got to get some women in there. Nice well rounded female characters with depth. Otherwise it's flat—just a bunch of blokes tossing off."

As they left he saw a dwarf sitting on the bar guzzling beer. He had seen him in the pub before and had never heard someone so foul mouthed. He was surrounded by grinning men, egging him on. They were probably amused by carousing with this small individual and were plying him with drink, unconcerned with his suffering and the damage they might be causing. There was something callous about it and he hurried outside to the street.

CHAPTER 23

At least two hours before Fabián was summoned to appear, he was required to bathe. First he would be fetched from his quarters and taken to the bath house by a group of men—all of whom were clean. They were both guards and guides. The palace was large. It was a city unto itself. He grappled to understand the sense he had that there was a ceremonial aspect to this summons. Aside from its obvious purpose of taking him to the king, it was a ritual as incomprehensible as the mind of a fly. His guides did not speak. All he could hear was the chirping of birds and the occasional roar of a beast beyond the walls. These were creatures from the king's collection, as was he.

It had taken him a few days to recover from the journey, which seemed a kind of madness to him now. He had slept for almost twenty-four hours in the room where they had put him. This was a strange imprisonment. He was mostly allowed to wander where he wished and was permitted to carry his dagger, except in the royal presence. No one mistreated him. He was not required to do any work. His lodgings were comfortable and he was well fed. Sometimes one of the palace women would secretly come and sleep with him.

He found this city an endless wonder. It surpassed anything he had ever seen. There was a large marketplace crowded with people, brimming with wares. There were flowers, spices, birds of different colours, vegetables and tools, textiles and objects carved from stone, sauces bubbling in pots. In the centre of the city were two temples sitting on mountains of steps. He was not allowed to go there.

Since he had arrived in Tenochtitlan people no longer died at his approach. Things had changed. He could only surmise that God was angry because of his frequent ablutions. This degree of cleanliness was obviously an unnatural vice, and he had allowed himself to be washed by half-naked women. Furthermore he had enjoyed it.

They scoured him with rough stones and ran their hands over him as he sat in half a fathom of warm water. After that a steam bath, sitting naked on a bench. Then clean clothes and an audience with the king.

The king was refined, exuding the confidence of someone who did not need to express his own power. Fabián had heard that he bathed eight times a day. On their first meeting, he sat at a chess table with Guillermo. The pieces were not set up in their correct positions.

The king sized him up with a glance. Fabián could feel it—an intelligence like a knife. He was being evaluated and felt himself lacking. He was ignorant of the protocols. Nobody had seen fit to inform him. He didn't know whether to bow or prostrate himself.

He stood with his gaze averted and waited. Guillermo stayed silent. They hadn't seen much of each other since they'd arrived. The king had given him a woman—the daughter of a high lord, and he was infatuated with her.

The king leant forward and said something. He was soft spoken and his words sounded polite.

"The Tlatoani greets you and wishes to know what this is." Guillermo indicated the chess board.

Guillermo would obviously know what it was and Fabián wondered why he had not already told him. What kind of trap was this? Then he realised that Guillermo was acting as an interpreter. He deferred to the king, and waited for him to speak first.

Around the room were numerous courtiers. From the fine feathered cloaks they wore, he assumed they were no mere servants.

"It is a game, Your Majesty. Popular in my country."

Was this the correct form of address? He felt his life hung on a thread but the king did not seem perturbed. He was talking again.

"He wants you to teach him how to play."

Fabián had learned chess young, from his older brother, and was a competent player. It was odd to see a chessboard in this place. If Guillermo hadn't brought it, then it must have been part of the long distance exchange of gifts between Cortès and the king. Cortès usually favoured giving away glass beads. They were cheap and plentiful. He would have the blacksmiths smelt the gold and silver artefacts he received in return and cast them into ingots. It seemed an unbalanced exchange but, if Guillermo was right, it was serving its purpose in luring the prey into the spider's web. It was only a matter of time before Cortès reached Tenochtitlan, and then what?

He started by resetting the pieces on the board. Then he named them and explained their moves and how the object of the game was to corner the opponent's king. Motecuzoma examined each piece. He spent a long time with the knight and the rook, turning them between his fingers.

After that Fabián had three audiences a week. There seemed to be thirteen days in a week, and eighteen in a month. It was complicated. Weeks and months had different significance and overlapped each other. Each visit was spent on chess instruction, and soon on playing. The king was a fast learner. Fabián tried to make sure he lost for fear of giving offence. His ruse had the opposite effect, as Motecuzoma saw through it and came as close to anger as Fabián had ever seen him. He spoke some words in an icy tone.

"Cowards and losers in battle are fed to the gods. On 1 Crocodile[1] you will play me for your life."

The woman Guillermo had been given was called Atotoztli, and she had become a fixture at the frequent chess games. Miraculously she was now able to speak a passable Spanish and acted as an interpreter with occasional help from Guillermo, who otherwise

---

1. 1 Crocodile. This refers to a specific day. The Aztec calendar consisted of two parts—*Tōnalpōhualli*, a cycle of 260 days divided into twenty thirteen day 'weeks', which was used for religious and ritual purposes. Each day was given a number and a symbol—hence 1 Crocodile. The other calendar, *Xiuhpōhualli* was Sun based and used agriculturally. Under this system the year was divided into twenty 'months' of eighteen named days and five unnamed days, making a total of 365 days. There have been differing scholarly opinions as to how these correlate to the Western calendar.

said little. Love had made him kinder and less self assured. Gone was his confidence and arrogance. His fear of losing her now took precedence over what he had been before.

Atotoztli was inscrutable and showed no emotion as she delivered the king's threat. Fabián was in a bind. If he lost he would die, and though he did not know the consequence of victory, he was sure it would not be good. Refusing the challenge was not possible. He had never played chess for his life before. He had never staked his existence on any game. He was afraid. It was hard for him to concentrate. He would surely die. Then no doubt he would stumble around purgatory, cold and lost, yet always expectant—of forgiveness and release, a faint hope that could never be reached. Hope was a punishment, a torture of indefinite postponement. Forever. Unless he had money. Then he could pay to have those sins dismissed. But he had none. That is why he had come to the New World. He was going to get rich. They all were.

He had lost his sense of time since he had been in Tenochtitlan. The days merged without definition. Everyone seemed to be aware of his upcoming contest, though nothing was said. It made him feel like a marked man and filled him with anxiety. The way these people measured their days made no sense to him and he did not know when to expect the arrival of 1 Crocodile. It came quite soon.

It was evident that this game would be different from any other he had played with the king. It was to be a culmination. A crowd of spectators gathered around them, maintaining a respectful distance—all high ranking lords and ladies, silent as the night. He sat opposite the king, his heart thumping, the empty board between them, the pieces set off to the side. Next came three priests, one of whom fumigated them with copal resin he carried in a brazier. A stream of devotions were uttered. Then a rook of each colour was removed and carefully wrapped in a small square of fabric. Fabián watched the process in growing dismay. His eyes were drawn to the long fingernails fumbling with the cloth. The wrapped pieces were placed in two identical boxes. The priests circled the board, passing the boxes between them as they went and reciting more verses from their scriptures. Finally they set down a box before each opponent and one of the priests opened them, the king's first. He was to play black. A courtier stepped forward to set up the pieces, mistakenly reversing the positions of the kings and queens. Motecuzoma scowled. The error was quickly corrected. Then the game began.

Fabián waited to make his first move. It had to be a good one. He wanted help. God had abandoned him. Maybe he should call upon His mother, or one of the saints, preferably one adept at chess. His lips moved in silent prayer and his mind began to clear. The king might be clever and precociously advanced for a beginner but he had only been playing for a short time. Fabián had years of experience. He was not the kind of player who calculated moves in advance, as he imagined the king to be. His style was more intuitive. He looked at the patterns the pieces made on the board and responded, but at the opening of the game there were no patterns. He waited, searching for an advantage. Then he had it. There were thirteen heavens in this place, and as he had recently learned, nine subterranean hells. Everything people did here was carried out in multiple domains. Everything had more than just one meaning. For him, chess was only a game. For the king it was a way to influence fate. He understood now. The king was also playing for his life.

He moved his king's pawn two squares into the open board.

Chapter 24

"WHAT ARE YOUR THOUGHTS?"

The sight of Fabian, awkwardly poised and out of sorts, reminded Dr French of that other Fabián at his last game of chess with the Emperor. Juanita was there, translating their anxious interjections, her serene face unmoved by their tension.

"I am thinking about the extended present, as described by Einstein, and how these seven minute sessions would likely last about twenty, were you to be here and I on Mars. Also, and more seriously, I am tormented by how my search for inspiration has extinguished it."

"Now that you have described your thoughts, tell me what you think thought is."

Fabian looked puzzled. "You are asking me what thought is?"

"Yes. What do you think?"

Fabian smiled at the double meaning.

"I would say a thought is a process rather than a distinct thing. And therefore it's a noun acting as many verbs in this case. Or to put it more simply—it's just something happening in your head."

"Are you sure it's happening in your head?"

"Well, I'm not particularly sure of anything but that's where the brain is, and if a thought is brain activity, then it's probably in the head, don't you think? What are you getting at?"

Dr French didn't know. It was just a way to seek relief from listening to details about the disappointing holiday in Mexico. He had shortened these sessions but even seven minutes were too long. A minute in eternity was torture.

"Would you say an idea is the same as a thought?"

"No. An idea is made of thoughts."

"So you could break an idea down into its constituent elements."

"I suppose so."

"Then ideas are compounds."

How times had changed. This Fabian, hunched on his seat, his elbows on his knees, was a man of his times, as were all men. Running water from a tap at whim meant little to him, as did illuminating a room with the single flick of a finger. Time made people as much as people made time. His own spagyric art had turned from science to the more abstract realm of psychology. He had watched the metamorphosis unfold over the previous two hundred years.

"What if thoughts were compounds as well? If you could do that to an idea, then you might be able to do the same thing to a thought and reduce it to its foundational elements—distilling its essence. You might call it pure thought."

It was all nonsense, spoken off the top of his head, though not completely groundless. He was drawing from that view of The Art popularised by the Victorians, where the transmutation of metals had been reinvented as an act of spiritual purification. The metals had come to represent human qualities. It was an idea that had served him well despite the fact that he didn't like it. Fabian appeared to take him seriously.

"Theoretically perhaps. But this all sounds very esoteric."

When he considered all the times through which he had lived, Dr French was amazed that civilisation still continued to function. Centuries of warfare, famine and disease had not yet been able to destroy it. He imagined there must be some underlying principle at work—a kind of cohesive fragmentation. That might explain his own predicament—being bound to existence but desperate to escape from it.

If he could only retrace his steps he would be able to die in poverty. He had never originally intended to live forever, or even to create unlimited wealth. He had just wanted to understand the workings of nature, and specifically the nature of matter. Curiosity had led him onwards and curiosity was boundless desire.

"In a state of ignorance, all things seem esoteric and arcane. It's dependent on relative position, as your philosopher Einstein would say."

"I'm not sure of your point."

"I'm suggesting a direction—a way to solve the problem that brought you here."

"What kind of direction is that?"

"It's long and arduous and roundabout. You'll have to be methodical and calculating, as you would with a Knight's Tour."

"I don't follow you."

"Do you play chess?"

"Not very well, but yes I do. On occasion."

He wondered if he was underestimating Fabian, who might be quick witted enough to understand he was being told nonsense. He had underestimated his namesake in Mexico, never considering him particularly remarkable until he saw him at the chessboard, where he had revealed a surprising acuity. Of course the stakes had been high. Fabián had been a good teacher, too. Motecuzoma had learned quickly and soon became obsessed with the game. He began to play it constantly, to the detriment of his other affairs. Each piece was significant to him. He saw the games he played as analogous to the events around him. It ended when he was murdered on the roof of his palace, stabbed from behind by a man from the Alvarado faction. They blamed his death on his own people, saying they had stoned him. Cortès was adept at his own self-serving propaganda, despite his mediocrity in other regards. The history of those times, still regarded around the world as truth, was written with his pen and by his own hand.

Dr French could not escape his memories.

"The Knight's Tour is an age-old mathematical problem, whereby you must calculate the sequence of moves so that the knight lands once on every square of the board."

"But I don't understand how this applies to me."

"You will, but it will take time. You came to me because you have lost direction, and you just said that your search for inspiration has extinguished it. I told you before that you are using your art to compensate for earlier psychic wounds. That is why I questioned you on your opinion of the constitution of thoughts."

"You are speaking in riddles."

Of course he was speaking in riddles. He had no intention that Fabian should understand him. The desire for direct comprehension was an idiotic fallacy. All these mortals assumed they had a right to comprehension. It was from undefined spaces that truth could seep. And only through effort. Had he not pondered similar riddles himself in times past? He had tortured metal for years in his workshop in Cordoba. Things are not what they seem. They just seem to be what they are.

"Habitual thoughts follow the same course, as a river constrained by its banks. It is difficult to make changes. When thoughts are reduced to their foundational elements—to pure thoughts—they are in a neutral state, in which all thoughts are potentially the same thought. What differentiates them are things that are added to the original state. Imagine three glasses of water on a table, all equally clear. Then add to them a drop of tincture—a different colour for each glass. Now they are no longer in a neutral state. In this way you can accomplish the transmutation of thought. You just have to discover the process of reduction and decide upon the tincture."

"It sounds like alchemy to me."

"Yes. That's an apt metaphor."

His patient had no real understanding of alchemy. Most people didn't, seeing only the image of an itinerant immortal, half charlatan, half wizard wandering the byways of Bohemia. How far from the truth they extended themselves. Chrysopoea had never been the intention of alchemy. Medicine was always a part of it with the quest for a universal panacea, but not for eternal life. Fate had led him to discover that secret at the end of the Silk

Road, where he met a fellow practitioner who had learned how to create the Chinese elixir. His own arrogant curiosity had led him to wheedle it out of the man. He had written down the formula in his book, using the code he had devised.

Fate had changed. It was once an edifice constructed by an invisible being. Now it appeared more random, with no particular intention, yet still retaining a fickle intelligence. Fate had become chance. It was the modern compartmentalisation of knowledge that allowed such a devaluation. Every era had its individual consciousness. He could remember the time when analogy and metaphor were not merely literary devices but forces of nature. Science today shunned such concepts and required proof through careful experimentation with exact measurement but in that regard it barely differed from alchemy.

"I don't understand how you add a drop of tincture to a pure thought."

"Our time has expired. We shall have to continue next week."

CHAPTER 25

IT WAS POSSIBLE THAT his doctor was mad. His ideas had a faint mediaeval quality, like a waft of frankincense.

How could you reduce a thought to its purest essence? What had he been talking about? Beneath the veneer of profundity, it didn't make much sense.

But perhaps there was some inadvertent benefit to Dr French's metaphysics. He was beginning to feel inspired again after the anticlimax of Mexico.

He had looked into the Knight's Tour and found a diagram showing the moves, not as a knight would actually make them, with combinations of the straight and diagonal, but as lines drawn between the centres of the affected squares. It produced a lattice of angles, denser on the outer edges of the board and strangely thin in the middle, like a wreath. Not so strange perhaps, as the starting position of a knight was towards the corner on the outer row. The importance of the starting place, as obvious as it might be, was an idea that applied to many subjects beyond the game of chess. Class structure for one.

Was this the reduction of thought that Dr French had been talking about, or was it just association?

It was dawn, the cleanest time of day. He lay in bed, thinking about the perception of time and how it could be expressed artistically. It could be a film, or a book. He would call it Novel Historical—a story that is told backwards. Revelation in reverse.

Whatever the format, it could play out in five minute intervals. Each five minutes would be used to describe what had happened in the previous five minutes. It would delve forever downwards and backwards. He considered mining as a metaphor, but mining always had a purpose—to seek out and extract. Who would mine just for the sake of digging a hole? This was more a peeling back, as in the removal of the skin of an onion, or starting at the end of a book and reading it all the way to the beginning. History would gradually reveal itself, though in such small increments that at first the past could scarcely be distinguished from the present. He might have finally found a way to express Einstein's concept that had so impressed him years before. As time goes by events recede from the observer. Each scene would end towards the beginning of the previous one. The five minute sections would run in reverse collectively, but individually they would play forwards. It would be like descending a staircase taking one backwards step up for every two steps down. It strained his imagination to follow such a thread.

The telephone was ringing. He looked out of the window at the orange band of light rising above the rooftops. Dawn and the telephone did not go well together. Who could be calling at this hour?

"3240, hello?"

There was no one there. The caller had hung up.

"3240, hello?"

There was no one there. The caller had hung up.

CHAPTER 26

FABIÁN, THE STRANGER WITH the hairy arms, had made his first move. The Tlatoani responded quickly, as if without thought, mirroring the move of his opponent. He had told her beforehand that this game would be important. He had never bothered to explain why. He hadn't told her the rules either, as if she didn't need to know but she had worked them out herself by watching and listening.

Atotoztli had surprised everyone by learning to speak the language of these foreigners. She seemed to have a skill with languages that even she found surprising. The Tlatoani was pleased. It was Guillermo who had taught her. He had also been teaching her other things, which he did not want her to talk about. While she sat by the chessboard speaking two languages, he had been cooking something in a sealed pot, which he called the egg. It had been on the fire for nine days.

The stranger called Fabián moved another pawn and the Tlatoani took it immediately with one of his own. As he removed it from the board his fingers expressed the pleasure his face did not reveal. Not a word was spoken. There was nothing to translate.

She wondered what needed to cook for nine days. Women did all the cooking. Girls learned it young. She was as competent as the rest but she'd never heard of anything that had to be cooked for so long. Guillermo said it was almost ready but would need to cool for a few more days. He was making it just for her, and he wanted her to have it before the other strangers arrived, which would be soon. He said it would make her live forever. He was not like other men. He knew things other people did not. He also had the unusual talent of being able to carry out different tasks with each hand at the same time. Most of what he said was incomprehensible. She didn't know what he meant by forever.

"Forever," he said, "is the love between us."

Whatever he meant, she knew his feelings were stronger than hers. He could not bear for them to be apart and followed her like a child. It was as if he saw in her the relief from loneliness, something she had never experienced herself. The only time he was not by her side was when he tended his cooking pot, or when he shared secrets with the Tlatoani. There was a connection between them. In public he was deferential but she suspected that when they were alone together they treated each other as equals. The Tlatoani knew how to be a ruler, a priest and a leader of men in war but Guillermo's knowledge went beyond these things, to places remote and strange, as if he could stride between the heavens. He told her he was old enough to be her ancestor. He was roaming the world when the eagle perched on the cactus, with the snake in its beak.

Fabián moved his bishop and the Tlatoani responded by making a long sweeping line with his queen, almost to the edge of the board, and threatened the white king.

"Check." He used the stranger's language.

Fabián moved his king out of harm's way, but she knew that he had lost the initiative and she could tell from his face that he knew it too. After that his attacks were defensive acts. He tried to push the black queen back to where she came from. This became a kind of dance, with threat and counter threat. Then Fabián lost one of his bishops, and soon after that both his rooks. The Tlatoani was moving in on his prey.

Suddenly one of Fabián's knights, that had been lurking in the middle of the board, sprang forward and checked the black king. Then he moved his queen to threaten the Tlatoani again, but in his haste to save his own life, he threw her away. She was taken by a knight. The Tlatoani smiled. The taste of victory was on his lips.

But what she had taken as haste on Fabián's part, she now realised was a ruthless plan. He had been sacrificing his pieces, especially the queen, to distract the Tlatoani, who, convinced of victory, did not see the last remaining white bishop that Fabián slid into position. There was no escape. The black king was trapped by the bishop and the knight.

"Checkmate."

The game was over. The king was dead.

The Tlatoani got up from the board and walked away. He had lost his empire and now must await the inevitable in whatever form it might take. She could feel a great change coming.

The inevitable arrived on 7 Crocodile in the form of General Cortés and his men. The Tlatoani and some eagle warriors went out to greet them on the causeway. She was among the crowd that gathered to watch. Some of the foreigners were seated on horses—creatures she had never seen before aside from the chess pieces, though Guillermo had told her about them.

The meal Guillermo had been cooking was ready and he cracked the egg. The shards of the pot were covered in a sticky black substance. He scraped away at it with his dagger until he found what he was looking for and handed her a small ball, the kind a dung beetle might carry on its back.

"Don't chew. Just swallow it with some water."

She was shocked by the small portion. She had expected something more substantial. But nothing surprised her about Guillermo for long. She took the ball with her thumb and forefinger and held it under her nose. It had no smell. She didn't feel inclined to eat it but she put it in her mouth anyway and swallowed it with the help of some water. It left a faint bitter taste that lasted a few days, no matter what else she ate.

By the time that bitterness had left her mouth, she had begun to feel different. She was thinking in a way that would have been inconceivable before. She started to question the assumptions she had grown up with. What would happen to her if she could never die, when the gods destroyed the fifth sun? They surely would one day. They would do it with earthquakes. How could she exist without a world?

The way she experienced time began to change. Believing that she would never die made it less important. She realised then that time was linked to the life and death of a body, an idea that had never occurred to her.

Now that his countrymen had arrived in Tenochtitlan, Guillermo was worried that she would be taken from him and insisted that they get married. They would take her name away and give her a new one. She felt a growing frustration with being moved around like one of those pieces from the game the Tlatoani could no longer bring himself to play. She was a noble woman who would live beyond the destruction of the fifth sun. She felt entitled to her own opinions and to act on them. This was not the attitude she had been brought up with. Penalties for any deviations were always severe. Death was a distinct possibility for those who drank too much pulque. Not that she drank pulque or had to worry about death anymore but Guillermo had made a point in telling her that though she would never die after eating the black pellet, which he called the Chinese Elixir, she could still be injured and should take all the normal precautions as if she was a mortal.

Cortés seemed mistrustful of Guillermo, or jealous, because he had come to Tenochtitlan first and because he knew the Tlatoani. She could tell he wanted to be in control of the situation—not an easy task as the allegiance of his men did not seem directed solely to him. But he managed it with his smooth tongue. Little did they know they were all prisoners here, alive only due to the grace of the Tlatoani, whose ear Cortés constantly sought. He demanded gold, which the Tlatoani gave him, at first in the form of precious objects. The temples were stripped of their treasures and the people grumbled. This could not end well. Later the foreigners were given lumps of gold, which Guillermo was making in secret. He knew how to make gold from other metals. He taught her how to do it too, and she helped him.

Guillermo was in a cantankerous mood. He complained that he did not have the high quality materials he needed. Imperfections in the salts he had used to make the elixir would cause her to remain childless. They would only have each other until the end of time.

It was a daunting prospect.

Chapter 27

Upon their arrival, the Castilians had been housed in a separate complex near the beasts and deformed humans. The emperor had managed to manipulate them into his collection without them knowing it, but soon after that he had moved in with them. It was an odd thing for such a powerful man to give himself up as a hostage, especially as he had been so successful in his plan to lure them to Tenochtitlan. Cortés said they had become close friends and Motecuzoma wanted instruction in the true religion. Fabián suspected that it was the fateful game they had played that had caused him to act that way. He might have wished to spare his people from a war he had already lost.

Whatever the reasons, he had become a part of his own collection. He began to play chess again with Cortés, having renounced it for some time. Fabián wondered if this was another attempt to influence events but none of their games had the same importance as the one he had played with the Emperor. They all had the fickle quality of just passing the hours. He began to think that God must have decided to use him for his skill at chess rather than as a bearer of disease. This would gather more souls, and the new kingdom would need labourers and slaves if it was to prosper.

Cortés let it be known that he had taught the Emperor how to play chess. It angered Fabián that such a brazen lie came from the lips of the man in charge. It caused him to lose respect. He lost respect for himself as well. He looked back at his life. It had been one adventure after another, each one leading nowhere and amounting to nothing.

Despite his close friendship with Cortés, Motecuzoma kept mostly to himself, tended by his servants who were all of noble birth. It seemed that he did not like the company of commoners.

Outside the palace the people were restless and becoming surly. Cortés warned against complacency and gave orders that the men should be drilled daily and that arms should be kept in a constant state of readiness—blades sharpened and oiled, crossbows and arquebuses cleaned, powder kept dry. The tension simmered.

Since he had beaten the Emperor at chess, Fabián had been shunned by the palace staff. There were no more baths, no more royal audiences, no nocturnal visitations. He had been left to his own devices. His fellow soldiers viewed him with suspicion as if he was a deserter.

Cortés summoned him and asked him to account for himself. He usually extended a welcome to those who had returned to the fold. He was interested in any intelligence they might provide.

Fabián couldn't give him much. He wasn't the kind of person who went around with an eye open for military intelligence. His journey to Tenochtitlan had been a fever dream. He hadn't noticed anything. Cortés was unconvinced but let him go and he went back to an uneasy existence with his former comrades, though on Motecuzoma's insistence he still slept in the room he had been given when he first arrived and did not share their quarters, which only increased their distrust. Cortés was happy enough to agree, hoping perhaps it might be useful in discovering palace intrigue.

Fabián felt that he had made a grievous mistake. He just didn't know what it was. God, the Virgin and the Saints had abandoned him. Guillermo was rarely present. No one trusted him. He sometimes saw Atotoztli but she was aloof and never spoke to him. He was lonely.

Atotoztli had become useful as a translator and Pedro de Alvarado had his eye on her. Cortés had La Malinche. Why should he not have a translator too? Fabián suspected that he also wanted to take her away from Guillermo out of vindictiveness. Beneath his affable handsome exterior he was ruthless and cruel.

Hoping to prevent Alvarado from taking her from him, Guillermo married Atotoztli in front of a cross bedecked with flowers in one of the palace courtyards. Motecuzoma and Cortés witnessed the ceremony along with other dignitaries, both Spanish and Mexican. Alvarado was noticeably absent. She was given the name Doña Juanita.

Rumours had been going round that Guillermo knew how to make gold. He kept it all himself, people said, and didn't give the king and his officers their rightful due as was the law concerning gold discovered in New Spain. This made him a traitor and a criminal, lacking in moral fibre, only to be expected from a magician in thrall to the Devil.

Guillermo's position was rapidly becoming more untenable, especially among Alvarado's faction. It seemed to mirror the growing tension outside the palace walls, a cascade of events tumbling towards catastrophe.

Then word came that an army sent by Velazquez to arrest Cortés had landed. They were under the command of Narvaez and had taken the city of Cempoala. Cortés assembled two hundred and sixty men and rushed to face them.

Late that night Fabián was roused from a deep sleep. Guillermo stood over him.

"Wake up!"

"What?"

"I need you to keep this for a while."

He dangled a linen bag over the bed.

"Give it to Juanita as soon as you can."

"Why don't you give it to her yourself?"

"Because she was ordered to do translation work and hasn't returned."

Fabián understood. Alvarado had taken her. Now that Cortés had left he was in command and could act with impunity. He loved only war and personal gain. He no doubt desired to see if there was any truth to the rumour about Guillermo's alchemical abilities. He would use torture, as was his custom. This bag must contain damning evidence. It was not something he wished to possess, but before he could refuse Guillermo had dropped it on the bed and disappeared.

Fabián lit a candle and looked inside the bag. It contained a book. He flipped through the pages. They were full of strange, nonsensical words and symbols. It could be a death sentence to be discovered with this. He quickly put it back and wrapped it in some clothing. He had been left with incriminating evidence and had been given no choice. A horrible thought dawned on him. On that nightmarish walk to Tenochtitlan, he had not been serving God, but the Devil.

In the morning Guillermo was arrested. While Cortés was in Tenochtitlan he was afforded some protection, as despite being mistrusted he was valued as a source of information. With Cortés absent, Alvarado could do as he pleased.

It was said that John the Bastard had run him through with a sword and when they went to dispose of the body, there was no body.

Chapter 28

As I WRITE THIS story, I am beset with doubt. There are so many books, so many voices. Expression is revered. Everybody wants to be heard.

When does all this expression become information pollution?

The lizard and its replica
Tried hard to understand
The differences between them
And distances by land

They came upon a notebook
Which offered only hope
They feasted on a paragraph
As permanent as smoke

In punctuated silence
They thought of many things
Of miles, minutes, millipedes
Of soap and puzzle rings

They pondered on the meaning
Of sand that was not there
In cabinets of darkness
As solid as the air.

Chapter 29

THE DOCTOR-PATIENT RELATIONSHIP REQUIRED intimacy with a stranger and made him feel awkward and displaced. He sensed that by some Archimedean principle, the familiar would recede proportionally as the unknown approached. This was the day he had agreed to ingest Delysid.

A few weeks earlier, Dr French had mentioned a new treatment to consider, a drug that might speed up the therapeutic process. With his usual alchemical metaphor, he had referred to it as the elixir.

"Will it make me live forever?"

"I doubt it. But if it did, I wouldn't recommend it. Aside from avoiding death, what is the attraction to immortality?"

Delysid was the pharmaceutical marketing name of lysergic acid diethylamide. Dr French had suggested it, but what did he know of Dr French? Nothing. So much was dependent on the trust of abbreviated titles. He had the creeping suspicion that fraudulence was the foundation of all civilised life, including his own.

He had been slipping into depression since his return from Mexico. It was like the gradual onset of a degenerative disease. It might have started earlier with the tepid reception of his film, *The Theory of Five Thousand Footsteps*. He hadn't noticed it much at first beyond a feeling of ennui and general listlessness. Then he started to think about the threshold between contentment and dissatisfaction. One day he found himself on the other side.

His ideals appeared to him now as baubles rather than shining orbs. His self expression did not even feel his own. He had thought he was destined to make films but ideas no longer came to him.

What had driven him to want to make films anyway?

He had read that Delysid could produce terror in some cases. His current state of mind did not seem particularly suitable for a jump into the unknown. He was afraid of his own fear. It seemed a natural enough emotion, though fraught with cowardice. Should he take the drug? What was there to lose but everything?

It seemed a grim logic that led him on. Freedom was limited by choice. Lack of choice was its own dull prison.

He decided to take the Delysid and regretted the decision while making it.

Dr French had removed a pill bottle from his desk drawer and was carefully shaking out a tablet on to a white porcelain saucer. He got up and rounded the desk, placing the saucer on the side table by Fabian, on which also rested a glass of water. It looked as if it had been there forever.

"Have you taken this yourself?"

"Just place it on your tongue and swallow it with a drink of water."

Dr French was never willing to answer personal questions but he felt no compunction about asking them of others. It was a kind of hypocrisy, a betrayal of the Hippocratic Oath.

If only to put an end to his doubts, Fabian did as instructed and swallowed the pill, punctuating the act with the thump of the water glass as he set it back on the table. He leaned forward, his elbows on his knees. Dr French had returned to his desk and was busying himself with his notebook and pen.

There was a self-conscious silence in the room—no sound but the faint hum of traffic from outside and the ticking of a clock.

"What are you thinking?"

Fabian had always hated that question—one which had been asked of him many times. The last bastion of privacy was the mind. If that was breached, there would be nowhere left to go.

"I'm thinking about being asked what I'm thinking about."

Most of what he was actually thinking about was mundane —the itch above his eyebrow, the gaps between buildings, a suit at the dry cleaners.

Light was bouncing off reflective surfaces, emanating from little, glowing embers scattered across the room. The beams they emitted were bristling, solid rods which made a tangled grid as they crossed each other. He would have to contort himself to climb through them. The drug had taken him by surprise. Its effect was strange. He had never seen things this way before. It was not unpleasant, though he felt a pressure in his head, and his mouth was dry. He reached for the glass of water beside him. The act of reaching had a feeling to it—slyly hesitant and surreptitious. When he raised the glass to his lips, he was shocked to see that the water was alive. The liquid was a writhing mass of white, eyeless larvae. He felt a horrible revulsion and let the glass fall from his hand. It shattered into thousands of crystals on the floor, releasing the creatures which crawled away with surprising speed. Then an understanding came to him, so sudden and pleasing that it made him laugh.

"I know what the trinity is."

"And what is that?"

He had forgotten that he was not alone. He glanced across the room—a great divide. Dr French looked wizened and ancient. In fact his head was a skull. The words left his mouth like sunlight refracted in a lens—rectangles increasing in size the further they travelled.

"It is two things with one thing in between them."

He could taste the words, sour like lemon. He glanced up at French to see if his head was still a skull. The empty eye sockets stared back at him. They were unbearable to look at and made him gasp.

French had risen and was coming towards him. Then he stopped and perched on the front of his desk. Fabian shrank back into his chair.

"You are frightened, Fabian."

Dr French was worse than the personification of death. In his living being were other living beings, each one a form of decay, gnawing with the ruthless constancy of insects at their alien purpose. He could not look, yet was trapped in a morbid fascination that forced him to keep raising his head, then made him cry out in terror and lower his gaze again to escape it. The floor was melting, and oozing away from him. It flowed over French's feet which were the talons of a bird of prey.

"In dreams and hallucinations you must approach what you fear, not run from it."

Fabian could not speak. He pulled his legs up onto the chair and hugged them. He peered down at the roiling floor. The surface was buckling and bubbling, an undulating gelatinous ocean that occasionally split open, revealing chasms that stretched far below him.

The floor was the surface of an illusion. Even illusions were illusions.

"I have something which might help you."

French was holding a circle. The rods of light did not impede him as he crossed the room. He passed right through them, his boney hands extending from the rags he wore.

Fabian's fear was pulsing. As he clasped himself in his chair, his limbs became the roots of trees. But something was beginning to change. The rods of light had become a glow of salmon pink, rising and expanding. It was dawn. He unclenched his body with relief and put down his feet to test the floor, which felt hard and secure again. The light had a sweet, faint sound. He relaxed back into his chair, allowing warmth to suffuse him. The sound grew louder and louder, until it made sense. The dawn was music.

"It's beautiful."

"Beethoven's Sixth Symphony—the Pastoral Symphony." French stood by the bookshelf. He no longer had a death's head.

Now that he knew he was listening to music he could appreciate its structure—a moving series of interlocking shapes that kept combining and recombining—sometimes into similar forms with slight differences, and sometimes surprisingly new. He watched as one moment became the next. The beauty flowed through him, but there was sadness to it. The sadness made him happy.

Suddenly the music stopped. Dr French lifted the stylus from the record and returned to his desk, sitting back in his chair and looking Fabian in the eye.

"It gets a little strident—not a good idea right now."

The abrupt silence was jarring, as if he had been shaken from a dream.

"Beethoven was a turbulent man. As a child, his insomniac music teacher forced him to wake up in the middle of the night for lessons. Imagine waking from a deep sleep and having to play the piano."

He imagined a piano—a grand piano. A large, sleek, black ungainly object, curved and straight, poised in a room, filled with the latency of sound. How could anyone make such a thing, or even conceive of it?

"Was Beethoven a friend of yours?"

French smiled, which was something he rarely did.

"I'm glad to see you are feeling better. Heaven and hell are the same place, you know."

Chapter 30

AFTER THE LSD SESSION, Fabian sequestered himself. He craved silence. He stayed in his flat, going out only to get supplies from the shop on the corner.

The proprietor was an old woman named Mrs Jones. She was amenable to opening packages and selling the contents in small amounts—a single slice of cheese, four pieces of bread, three cigarettes, a slice of bacon. Fabian liked that about her and only bought what he needed for the day, though it was never bacon. That meant he had to go out every morning.

Mrs Jones didn't often have many customers and it was usually just the two of them when he went in. Their encounters involved cursory good mornings, the recitation of a brief shopping list, money on the counter, the ring of the till. Then it was back home with a paper bag.

He kept returning to the image of Dr French as living death. He couldn't dispel the idea that he had seen the doctor for what he truly was. The drug had laid bare the being beneath its trappings.

Within that being was another, and in that yet another—a series of Russian dolls, diminishing into a molecular vibration that had an intelligence all its own and followed different laws.

He retrieved the book he had stolen in Mexico and set it on his desk. He would make another attempt to understand it. He was bored and had to keep busy. But as he studied the pages he found himself questioning the need to be always doing something.

He took his cane and went out to Mrs Jones' shop. The bell tinkled as he entered, as it always did, making him uneasy for a moment. There was a man at the counter, a big man. He didn't appear to be buying anything, just talking. He stepped aside as Fabian approached.

A hint of relief flickered in Mrs Jones's eyes as she interrupted her conversation to take his order. She had obviously talked more than she wanted with this man at the counter. By the time Fabian's order had been bagged, he was gone.

"Is he a relative of yours, Mrs Jones?"

"No. And I'd stay away from him if I were you."

She was not prepared to say more, despite his curiosity. He grasped his cane and made his way out, clutching the bag under his other arm. When he reached the door it opened before him.

"Thank you."

"Get that in the war did you?"

"Get what? The shopping?"

"The leg."

The big man let go of the door and extended his hand.

"I'm Johnny Burnham."

Fabian shifted the bag to his other arm and shook his hand. "Fabian Davis." He wondered why he was going along with this.

The situation was innocuous enough but Mrs Jones' warning was still fresh in his mind.

"Could you give us some help?"

In a flurry of embarrassment, Fabian reached for his wallet.

"No. Put it away. Put it away, mate. Not that kind of help."

"What do you need then?"

"I've got a little problem with the council. Tell you what, I'll buy you a pint and you can take a look at this letter." He tapped his coat pocket.

Fabian knew he was being played but not why or how. It was beginning to drizzle. He looked down at Johnny Burnham's shoes. Size thirteen, or thereabouts, slightly spattered. The trouser cuffs rode down on them, frayed at the back from being caught under the heel.

"All right. I'll have a quick one."

They crossed the road and went into the King's Head. It was almost empty inside. Johnny bought two pints and brought them over to the table by the window, where Fabian was sitting.

"Here you go."

"Thanks. Now what's this problem of yours?"

Johnny took the envelope from his pocket and set it on the table. Fabian tried to read the address but couldn't see it clearly.

"It's about my old mum. She's my angel. I couldn't stand to lose her. It almost killed her when I went on holiday."

"You were away long?"

"Five years. I just got back."

"At Her Majesty's pleasure?"

"Yes. The Scrubs. Free room and board for five years. A bargain."

Johnny Burnham hadn't touched the envelope since he had set it on the table and it lay there dormant. He lifted his glass and took a long sip, draining half of it and leaving a little foam on his lip, which he licked off.

"I was gone for five years during the war too, driving a lorry for the army."

He didn't seem in any hurry to broach his problem.

"There isn't a thief on earth that can match an Italian. You walk away to take a piss or something, come back a minute later and everything's gone. Even the wheels. Bits of the motor too. You've always got to leave someone on the lorry. But we found a way to fuck them. Oh yes we did. Want another pint?"

"No thanks"

Drinking beer in the morning blurred his mind. It was like finishing before starting. He wanted to see Johnny Burnham the way he had seen Dr. French, down through the surface—through the essential idea of the person into the vibration beyond. But he saw only the usual three dimensions. 'Johnny' seemed an incongruous name for a felon. 'Burnham' was more suitable.

"The way we did it was to sell them the stuff they were going to steal, or some of it anyway. We'd sell it to them, see... before they had the chance to rob us."

"Clever."

"It gets better, mate. It gets better. You see there were two of us on the lorry. One of us would take the money and the other would go round the back with a gun and relieve them of the goods they had just purchased. Then we'd fuck off. It worked like a charm. Every time. There's something glorious about stealing from a thief!"

Fabian wondered what Burnham had done to spend five years in Wormwood Scrubs, not a place he would wish to stay a single night. Its high, tightly packed brick walls and looming towers were the symbols of merciless justice.

"What do you need help with?"

"When I was away this letter arrived and Mum just left it, waiting for me to get home."

"You live together?"

"Yes...well, someone has to look after her, don't they? I can't count on my brother. He's away himself at the moment."

"What exactly is the problem?"

"The council want us out the flat. Due to my transgressions, see? They can't make her move. Not at her age. It's not right."

"Is that what the letter says?"

"Dunno."

"Have you read it?"

"No."

Fabian had been apprehensive when he agreed to have a drink but now he was beginning to enjoy this illogical conversation. It had the ring of Irish myth that he enjoyed so much. There was an inherent chaos in even the most banal situations. He had the sensation of warmth in his stomach. Perhaps it was just from drinking beer in the morning. Whatever the cause, he was less worried about being used for an unknown purpose, which probably concerned money—the foundation of most trickery. He didn't mind and was in fact looking forward to being cheated. He had his own ulterior motives.

"How do you know it's an eviction notice, if you haven't read it?"

"The neighbours have been talking. They want us out. They don't like me. They must have complained."

"If you were so concerned, why didn't you read it?

"That's why you're here, mate.... You see...I have certain troubles with the written word."

"You can't read?"

"Well...a bit. I can read numbers and that, but words is all snakes on the page, turning this way and that."

Fabian imagined inviting Burnham up to his flat and letting him have a crack at deciphering the book. There was a pleasing, symmetrical asymmetry to having an illiterate person break a code. But the idea was grotesque, cruel even. His cruel streak disturbed him.

"Let's have a look then."

Burnham slid the envelope over the table towards him. It was unopened.

"Want another pint?"

"No thanks."

"I'll make this worth your while. You'll see. You like *escargots*, mate?"

Snails were an odd form of payment. This was getting more interesting, and absurd too, like playing billiards with the pope.

"I got a taste for them when I was in France. Loved them. I can give you a lifetime supply. In tins."

"I haven't done anything yet. I don't even know if I can. But tell me, what made you think I could help you? Why did you pick me?"

"Like I said, I have trouble with the written word. But I can read faces. And in your case, legs. I'm the William Shakespeare of legs and faces. A fucking maestro."

He sprang from his chair and stood at his full height, which must have been about six foot five. Then he proceeded to impersonate an orchestra conductor, waving his hands in time to imaginary music. There was a frenzy to the act, a desperation expressed as joy.

Fabian picked up the envelope. It was from the Lambeth Metropolitan Borough Council. At least Burnham had that right. Maybe someone had told him.

"Let's see what this is about."

The envelope was pinched between his thumb and finger, but he paused before opening it.

"You still haven't told me why you think I can help you. I'm not a lawyer. Why didn't you ask someone you know?"

"I don't want anyone I know to know my business. I needed a proper gent. Someone who has a thumb in the invisible workings above. One of those public school boys but not the kind that just ponces about. Someone who's suffered as I have. You fit the bill. I can tell. You've been suffering. Not the way I have. But suffering is suffering."

He was a bundle of opposites, Johnny Burnham. A criminal with empathy.

"Okay, let's see what it says." Fabian tore open the envelope. Burnham waited in his chair, expectant and alert. Fabian glanced at him. He looked vulnerable and childlike. It was strange that all big people were small once. Then he read the letter. There were only two lines. He looked up with a grin.

"What does it say?"

"Apparently they are going to be turning off the water in your building for four hours in order to do some plumbing work."

"That's it?"

"Yes. And that was three months ago. Did they ever do the work? If anyone could turn four hours into three months, it would probably be a borough council."

"You know what I mean."

Fabian was puzzled. Was this a joke or a grammatical error? He couldn't tell.

"I think it would be better to say 'I know what you mean'."

"You do, do you?"

There was a menacing tone to those words and an ambiguity, which seemed intentional. He was obviously not a person who liked criticism, but then who did? The mirror structure of the phrase was clever—suggesting a dual meaning of anger and humour. It was quite poetic. It was a pity he didn't know how to write.

"I'm curious. What did you do that got you sent to prison? If you don't mind me asking."

Burnham smiled. He didn't seem at all ashamed of his criminality.

"Fraud, mate."

"Five years for fraud?"

"It involved a bit of money. Quite a bit."

CHAPTER 31

Fabian wondered if he still wanted to make films. He had only made one, aside from his government work. Was he to be a film director who never made films? Yet he was not certain he was ready to let go of his ambition. Without it his life would just be time spent waiting. He needed to diverge—away from orthodoxy. He would have to disregard everything he knew.

The thing to do would be to imagine a film without attempting to make it. He could direct his own imagination. It would be a bit like reality, a reverie surrounded by the unknown.

He ran through the scene of Burnham in the pub. It had a film-noir quality to it, with an ambiguous kind of humour, either funny or disturbing.

Burnham had pushed back his chair and jumped up, desperately imitating a conductor, tall and powerful—a thug who loved his mother. He could make something of that.

It was after ten—time to go out for supplies. He hankered for a boiled egg.

There was a cardboard box at the top of the steps outside. He bent down and saw that it was addressed to him—handwritten with no postage mark.

When he got back with his shopping, he heaved it up the stairs. It seemed much too heavy for a box that size. He dropped it by the leg of the kitchen table and cut it open.

It contained tins of snails. A lot of them. One gross as the note inside stated, signed JB. So Burnham had kept his word, but he had lied about being illiterate. This was an unexpected plot twist.

It turned out that Burnham was not who he appeared to be. He was in fact an aristocrat—Lord Burnley, who had run up gambling debts. He had presented a box of jewels to a pawnbroker in return for a loan over a specified period. During this time Burnley would make payments until the loan was settled and would then retrieve his jewels. This arrangement was not unusual for the pawnbroker who made a good living by discreetly assisting the upper classes.

After some months went by and he had received no payments, the pawnbroker opened the box again. It contained only lumps of coal. It wasn't difficult to track Burnley down and threaten him. Whereupon Burnley promptly appeared with a cheque to cover the loan, written by a good friend.

When the pawnbroker tried to cash it there was trouble. The bank baulked, and the friend denied ever having written it. The case went to court. Burnley was convicted of fraud and sentenced to five years in prison. Or was it six?

By the time his sentence was complete and he left Wormwood Scrubs, Burnley had reinvented himself as Burnham—a working class criminal. Then again, Burnham might always have been Burnham and had just lied about being Burnley.

The sleight of hand involved in switching out the box of jewels for an identical one, loaded to the same weight with coal, would have required a high level of competence. He would have needed perfect timing.

Or he might merely have leapt at an opportunity if one had arisen. Perhaps the pawnbroker had left the room for a few minutes to relieve himself.

What struck Fabian as odd was why it took the pawnbroker so long to look in the box again. Most people would have had another quick look as soon as Burnley had left the room.

It was possible that the pawnbroker inspected the jewellery and put it directly into his safe. If Burnley was present, he would have turned his back while opening the safe. He wouldn't want to risk revealing the combination. He might have needed both his hands. Burnley would have been holding the box. The pawnbroker's back was turned. That was when the switch took place.

Alternatively, there might have only ever been one box. In his shabby back room, the pawnbroker quickly appraised its contents. There were velvet drawstring bags of uncut stones, all of high quality, a large topaz set in a ring of fourteen carat gold, necklaces and bracelets encrusted with gems, and a cameo locket of a lady from former times, probably the beloved of one of Burnley's ancestors.

Moments later he declared a value. It was less than Burnley had expected. He then put the box in his safe and the papers were signed. There was no switch, no fraudulence.

Sometime over the next few months, whether suddenly or through slow and constant change, the jewels became coals. This magical transformation seemed to imply that the coals were retribution for a life of bad moral judgement. But who was the guilty party? Was it the pawnbroker for his opportunism? Or Burnley, addicted to gambling and blinded by his needs, a slave to himself? Maybe it referred to both of them, which is why the pawnbroker was left with nothing and Burnley did time.

This dramatisation of thought was a risky path and Fabian realised it could lead to obsession and madness, the way chess consumed some people. Like chess it had so many permutations and strategies and could ruin a life, but he was already absorbed and had no desire to abandon it. He could use this technique, if he ever made films again. It would be a cubist cinema.

CHAPTER 32

DURING THE FIRST FEW years of living forever, Juanita came to assume she was a goddess. What else could immortality mean?

She was not completely convinced about it until after she'd left Tenochtitlan. As she wandered, she knew she was a goddess. But which one? Ayauhteotl perhaps. That would explain her ability to come and go like the mist. Or she might be Chalchiuhticue, which is why she was so attracted to the lake and the snakes she found there.

People she met recognised her divinity and would supplicate, or flee in terror. To those who did not run she would utter prophetic statements, short and deliberately vague, inspired by the strange words Guillermo had used—alembic, cinnabar, salamander, sublimation. Those people's lives would be changed by meeting her in ways they would never understand.

She had managed to get away from Pedro de Alvarado in the confusion when they were crossing the western causeway. Guillermo had vanished the week before. That night she met

Fabián, who had brought on the disaster by beating the Tlatoani at chess. He thrust a bag into her hands.

"Take this. Your husband wanted you to have it."

There was fear in his eyes. He seemed desperate to get rid of the bag but trying to appear as if he wasn't. The rain poured down on them. That is how she came by Guillermo's book.

She made her way along the lakeshore, staying as far away from the Spanish as possible. They had been driven from the city and a lot of them had been killed, some drowning with their stolen treasure and their horses. They no longer seemed so invincible, though she knew they would return. The chess game had decreed it.

She came to understand that the only real difference between gods and mortals concerned time. For her it was insignificant, for them it was pervasive. Otherwise they shared the same emotions and needs. She needed shelter. She was lonely. Theoretically she did not need to eat. She could starve herself indefinitely and never die. But she ate anyway. Habit perhaps.

When she left Tenochtitlan she didn't know where to go. She had stayed away from Tlaxcala, where the Spanish went after their defeat. A war had raged for two years. Disease swirled around them, the city was retaken and destroyed, many people were killed or enslaved.

If she wanted to hide, it would be best to live among mortals. She would have to find another husband. It would be easier than wandering alone with the burden of beauty, even if she was a goddess, which she had now begun to doubt.

She was more likely just the wife of a magician who had disappeared. Guillermo's magic food had not turned her into a goddess even if it had made her immortal. It had stolen her sense of belonging. There was still a bitterness—not of taste but of separation.

She envisaged the future as an endless landscape through which she must pass—great planes of grass, layers of mountains receding into the sky, rivers, oceans, cities. It seemed there was nothing left but more.

Over twenty years she aged as a mortal woman but in her fortieth year she stopped growing older.

With trepidation she had gone back to Tenochtitlan. It had a different name. The temples of the Sun and Moon were gone. The Spanish had razed them and built themselves their own town within the city, which they called the Traza. They wouldn't let anyone in but their own kind. It was when the guards turned her away that she had met Fabiàn on his way out. He now owned a *hacienda* in the countryside and had just been granted an *encomienda*—the right to benefit from the labour of the local people without having to pay them. He was in an expansive mood.

It was a lucky meeting. He wanted to show her his new farm. She went back with him and stayed there until he died thirty years later. It was an easy transition. In a short space of time she had begun to live as his wife, though he would not marry her because she already had a husband. Assuming that he did not know Guillermo's secret she had told him that her husband was most likely dead and she was free to marry again, but Fabián would not be budged. Without confirmation of Guillermo's death, he had to assume there was a chance that he still lived. Perhaps he did know Guillermo's secret after all.

Even if they were free to marry, he feared it would anger another woman called Maria. It seemed unnatural to be so beholden to a woman who was not there. A grown man should not be so submissive. But then he said that this woman was the mother of the god they had sacrificed on the tree. She had helped him through misfortune, guided him through danger. She had never let him down. She loved him as a son, no matter his faults. Only she could forgive him for allowing himself to be deluded by the Devil, who was masquerading as God.

That was when he had been travelling to Tenochtitlan with Guillermo. He had been suffering from ague for most of the journey and had believed that he had been chosen to spread disease as an incarnation of Xipe Totec. It was Guillermo who had encouraged him in this falsehood. He had become dangerously close to abandoning the true religion. In his opinion Guillermo was a necromancer in thrall to Baphomet. Yet it was to him that he owed his life. Nothing was straightforward.

He rarely spoke of these things and she knew he didn't like to think about them. They contradicted the story he wanted to believe about himself. He never mentioned the bag he had given her with Guillermo's book, as if by reticence he would consign it to nonexistence.

The experiences of capture and imprisonment, of dreams and battles, of wagering his life on a game of chess, had taken something from him. He was lacking in malevolence and cruelty, his doubts gave him depth. She liked that about him.

She had neither liked nor disliked Guillermo. Their marriage had nothing to do with her. He had decided upon it with the

Tlatoani. She had simply been carried along by the power of law and custom.

Guillermo had given her eternity, whether she wanted it or not. He was arrogant about his abilities. Fabián was not arrogant at all. His voice was soothing and sweet, though at times he could be stubborn. She helped him administer the farm, and as she had better organisational skills, she took on more of the work until eventually she was running it by herself. That left him free to enjoy his wealth. It bothered her that they were getting rich from the toil of her vanquished people. Yet she kept doing what she did.

She enjoyed the comfort of their life together—the weight of his arm flung across her in his sleep, the smell of his skin. The time would come when she would have to leave all of this. Fabiàn was growing older; she was not.

Freed from the burden of managing his property, Fabián spent his time entertaining. He liked talking to educated men—it was mostly men who enjoyed his hospitality. More Spanish women had been arriving from across the sea, now that the war was over, and some would occasionally attend. They seemed haughty. Perhaps it was because they disapproved of their men taking up with native women. It was always at the back of her mind that Fabián would one day choose a wife from one of these new arrivals. It was a nagging worry but it would probably not change their arrangement. He seemed very happy with what she offered him.

From conversation at the table one night, she heard that Cortés had killed his own wife. It was apparently the talk of the Traza but no one could be certain if he was guilty. They talked about how Velasquez would react, seeing she had been his kinswoman.

The talk was capricious, aided no doubt by numerous bottles of wine. Despite the disdain of the women, the men accepted her quite naturally, and as she was of noble birth they had given her the title Doña. She preferred to listen rather than talk. The conversation turned from the potential murder of Cortés' wife to something which interested her more—the roundness of the world.

The Greeks, who appeared to be their ancestral people, in the same way as the Toltecs were to the Mexica, had come to the opinion that the world was round many years before and the idea had been confirmed by seafarers. She was of course aware of the thirteen heavens and nine subterranean worlds with mortals living between them but she had never equated them with any particular shape. To think of the whole thing as round had an instant effect on her—a kind of trepidatious excitement and wonder, with a tinge of doubt. She was to feel those same emotions hundreds of years later, when she was first introduced to the telephone.

That idea of roundness had a quality to it like salt of hartshorn and brought on a flurry of unrelated thoughts. She began to think of greed. She had helped Guillermo make gold to give to the Tlatoani after the temples had been stripped bare. The Spanish could never be satisfied. Whatever they received, they wanted more. Why had he obliged them? It was after the chess game and he was no longer able to contain them.

The Tlatoani had been greedy too. It was the tribute flowing into Tenochtitlan that had made the city so rich and powerful. Greed was a condition that afflicted mortals, some worse than others. It came as naturally to them as the need to eat. They had to ascribe value to a thing in order to desire it, and they had to desire it in order for it to have value. That was the roundness of greed—to chase something and never catch it—a futile pursuit that had become so ingrained it was a way of life. She knew that just as she had hidden among mortals for the sake of convenience, she could float on their river of greed. It was only with the eventual advent of newspapers that she began to understand how that could be done.

Before she and Guillermo could be married she had to accept their new god. It wasn't hard to oblige. New gods arrived from time to time from other cities. It was not unusual. She had to take instruction from their priests. They told her that they had come here to save everyone. There were no other gods but their own. She had been living in error and worshipping devils.

She didn't much like the idea of only one god. And anyway this one seemed to be three gods, or four if you included the mother, but the priests assured her there was only one. The three or the four were one.

They said people who accepted him as the only true God would live forever. She was already living forever, so they were wrong about that and her adherence was only skin deep. They were always suspicious that those who professed belief were secretly continuing their old ways and were wont to burn people they distrusted. She didn't have to worry about death but pain, humiliation and maltreatment were a distinct possibility.

There was one visiting priest, who was different from the rest. He was scathing about the way her people were treated. He had given up his own *encomienda* and urged Fabián to do the same. He was a brave man, speaking out about the injustice he saw, and he gave her the hope that one day she would find her own way to right these wrongs. The other *encomenderos* considered him dangerous; they knew he had the king's ear. She feared he might go the way of Cortés' wife. Nothing was too sacred to escape elimination should necessity demand it. Justification was always an afterthought.

Fabián had become an old man. His voice quavered and he moved about slowly, grunting when he stood from his chair. She was still forty. She had expected him to say something about her perpetual youthfulness but he never did. Perhaps he already knew about her immortality. Guillermo had given him his precious book, so they might have talked, or he could have intuitively grasped it without knowing what it was he understood. Maybe he just didn't care. He was an unusual man. He owned a large farm but didn't seem concerned about heirs. Perhaps he intended to give it to her.

Fabián died in his sleep by her side.

She let her hand rest on his brow; his hair was stiff and lifeless. To see him age and die while she stayed young was unbearably sad. Without Fábian, there was no life for her on this farm.

That long awaited time had come.

She left before dawn and set out towards the north.

The year was 1562.

CHAPTER 33

Burnham stood by the curtain and looked down into the street.

"Do you see that man across the road?"

Fabian got up from his desk and moved over to the window. There were quite a few people in the street below.

"The one with the theodolite? What about him?"

"He's a spy."

"He's probably just a surveyor."

"That's what spies are."

Ever since their first meeting Fabian had found Burnham increasingly intrusive and annoying. He was frequently an uninvited guest. In the unlikely event that there was indeed a spy over the street and not just a surveyor doing his job, Burnham seemed to imply that he, Fabian, was the one being watched. If anyone was to be spied upon, Burnham seemed the more likely candidate.

Because of his experiments with making imaginary films, and allowing external and internal realities to mix, he had come to assume that Burnham was his own idea. Yet the idea had run off and left him in the dark. He was unsure about Burnham's reality. He was not even certain of his own. What if Burnham had a split personality and was two people? Burnham and Burnley. Then it was feasible that these two characters could be split personalities themselves, who in turn were split—a constant branching out like the tree of life, and he might find himself to be just an offshoot of one of Burnham's personae. The more one tried to define reality, the harder it became. The answer he realised was quite simple, if counterintuitive—reality was an aggregate of the unknown.

He could imagine a different scenario, something that would have happened earlier, which would culminate in this moment. It would be more dreamlike and shocking and it didn't have to make sense.

Burnham had been attacked by a wolf.

At the centre of Fitzroy Square was a garden, surrounded by wrought iron railings. The gate was locked. Burnham had vaulted the fence. Seconds later he was bitten by a wolf.

When he hobbled back to the flat he didn't notice a man standing in a recessed doorway holding bellows and watching him with quiet malevolence as he passed.

The idea had a brash sensibility. It was a breath of dark light.

"What makes you think he's watching me and not you?"

"What's that?" Burnham had turned from the window.

"What's what?"

"On your desk. That book."

"You're right. It's a book."

Fabian was annoyed with himself for having left it out. Seeing it lying open was a reminder of how he had acquired it. He had tried yet again to decipher it the night before and went to bed late, forgetting, or not bothering to put it away. Now it was exposed to Burnham's aggressive curiosity.

Burnham peered over his shoulder.

"What's it say?"

Fabian felt a burst of anger and disdain, the influence of Mercury in the First House.

"How the fuck do I know? Maybe you should give it a shot. If you can read."

"Down boy!"

Burnham broke into a big, generous smile which appeared to be genuine. Humour sparkled from his eyes. He made a calming gesture with his hands. It was an unexpected response. His face would often bristle with violence at the most inane comment, yet now when confronted with a direct attack he was amused and conciliatory.

Fabian knew that it was time to end his self imposed exile. He should call Helen. Her practical, down to earth intelligence would counter all these Russian dolls.

Burnham was looking closely at the book.

"Where did you get this thing?"

"That's a long story.... You know, there's blood on your leg."

CHAPTER 34

CHARLIE PHONED HIM AND they agreed to meet in Richmond Park for a walk. It wasn't a pastime he engaged in much as it caused him considerable pain these days. Charlie was the one who had suggested it.

He missed their collaboration. It had been so easy. They'd had a mutual understanding. Part of it was acceptance—of taking each other's ideas and building upon them, rather than denying them or trying to change them. That was a rare connection. He had never experienced it with anyone else.

His trip to Mexico had changed everything. He had come back a different person. They hadn't argued or fallen out but a silence had sprung up between them and their connection was lost. They were both swept away by different currents.

He suspected that Charlie felt the same way. They walked in uneasy silence, their attention drawn to a large herd of miniature deer grazing in the pasture below. Possibly a hundred, maybe more.

Charlie broke the ice.

"Do you mind if I put something by you?"

"By all means."

"There's a group of friends—in their late sixties or seventies. They meet once a week on Fridays to have supper together and talk. Though it's not as casual as it sounds. Their gatherings have an intellectual purpose. In some ways it's like Freud's Thursday Club, except there's no Freud, no chairman of the board. They consider themselves equals and treat each other with mutual respect."

"What links them together?"

"All of them have a certain defect."

"What sort of defect?"

"It's linguistic. When engaged in conversation there are certain parts of speech they cannot say. It's a kind of vocal dyslexia. That's what brought them together. They were individuals who suffered from a very specific mental disorder who found each other. These meetings sustain them.

"I like the sound of it."

"Their conversations can get quite interesting. I have a snippet from one Friday."

He unfolded a piece of paper he had taken from his pocket.

"I should explain—Carole Wasserman can't say proper nouns. Trevor Bart's problem is pronouns. Graham Foote is devoid of verbs. Anita Pole won't utter a common noun. This is a small segment from the evening when they were discussing Quietism. Here, you read it."

Fabian took the paper from him. They paused in the shade of a gnarled tree.

Carole: I've always been drawn to.

Trevor: To?

Graham: I she she to other people.

Carole: I was referring to a philosophy. The philosophy of.

Trevor: But do mean precisely?

Anita: I think she means Quietism—the that wants to solve the caused by.

Graham: It to humanity from the perplexity.

Carole: Exactly.

Fabian laughed. "Very promising. What have you got in mind for it?"

"Nothing specific. It was an experiment really. It could probably be improved. I have to make it more entertaining, more readily amusing. It's quite difficult to write that way. I was thinking it could be a radio programme. The BBC might be ready for something a little unusual. And what with Zlodyk[1] all over the papers, the public might be too. This is 1954—the Year of the Horse, after all."

"What do you make of him?"

"Who? Zlodyk? I just read that he always enters and leaves rooms backwards. I think it's brilliant—to enter somewhere backwards, to cross a threshold in reverse. It says so much. It's a simple physical expression of a complex profundity. It turns reality on its head, English middle class reality at any rate. That man's a genius."

---

1. Jaroslav Zlodyk was a Croatian artist and philosopher. See Appendix 3.

Fabian glanced down to a mysterious little forest of old trees, some distance away. There was a lurking figure. A large man in an overcoat. Burnham, damn it. Burnham was spying on him.

"What is it?" Charlie had noticed his sudden change of expression.

"It's nothing."

"No. Something's bothering you."

"There's a man down there among the trees. Suspicious looking. I think he's following us."

"Where?"

He pointed with his cane. "Down there."

They both looked. There was no one there. They were left with a remnant of doubt—an empty moment.

"I think your mind just ran away with a shadow, Fabian."

Chapter 35

He sat in the kitchen, his feet on the table, reading a newspaper article about Zlodyk.

Zlodyk followed his own arcane agenda, expressed in broken English, which seemed to explore the layer of meaning just below the obvious. The article was about his opinions on thresholds and egress. For him each door was a window of opportunity. The press didn't know what to make of him.

Fabian put down the paper. He admired Zlodyk. He was really quite subversive—just by being himself. But who had he been before he appeared in London? Had he reinvented himself?

Fabian had always felt that he had been invented by someone else. Maybe that is what prompted him to invent his conquistador namesake.

Though in reality he had not so much invented Fabián. He had just picked his name and his place and date of birth. Beyond that he had nothing to do with him. Maybe that's all it took—a name, a place and a birthdate.

His interest piqued, he reached into his desk drawer for the single sheet of paper on which he had started to interpret Fabián's chart. It had lain there untouched since he came back from Mexico. As he felt around for it he noticed that the book was missing. With mounting concern he fumbled some more. Perhaps it had been pushed to the back but he couldn't feel it there. He pulled the drawer out of the desk. It was gone.

With rising anxiety and a burst of doubt he wondered if he might have left it somewhere else in the flat. He tore about, throwing his pillows to the floor, pulling off the bed sheets, rummaging through papers and even searching in the most unlikely places like under the kitchen sink. All to no avail. He knew that he always kept it in his desk drawer. Someone had taken it. He had only left it out once as far as he could remember. That was when Burnham had stopped by.

It had to have been him. The bastard. He'd been overly curious in that way of his that had no respect for personal boundaries. He probably noticed its age and thought he could get some money for it.

Fabian sat down and surveyed the mess he had made. He hadn't seen Burnham recently. No doubt he was keeping a low profile after stealing the book. He would confront him. It was unfortunate that he didn't remember the address on that envelope in the pub but how was he to have known it would be important? Why was he so obsessed with this book anyway? It was irrational. But not so irrational perhaps. He had felt bad about taking it at the time and that feeling of guilt had never completely left him. Perhaps it had even pre-dated the theft and represented the way he had always viewed himself. It was a bad feeling that had transformed into something else, something much larger than personal guilt. Something archetypical—a wound perhaps, as retribution for moral turpitude. A wound in the groin, in the genitals, like the Fisher King. If he remembered correctly the wound had made the Fisher King impotent.

Since he had stolen it his life had changed for the worse. The film he had been planning escaped him. The principal character was leading his own independent existence. His imagination had been merging with his perception, making a mockery of reality. His mind was swirling with what he called the Russian Doll Effect where everything was inside everything else. *The Theory of Five Thousand Footsteps* had been prescient.

He saw the book as a symbol just as indecipherable as the fading script across its pages. He imagined it was a fulcrum of change. The kind of change that spiralled forever inward. Maybe he was better off without it. Yet he felt its loss. Being robbed was a violation but it was more than that. The Fisher King was cured when someone, Percival maybe, had asked the right question. Words had healed him.

Could it be that he believed that if he could decipher the book its words would heal his wound? The wound caused by stealing it? Was the solution to his problem the problem itself?

An impotent king could have no heirs. An impotent film director could make no films. In his case the impotence was symbolic, not physical, as Cynthia[1] could attest, but it had the same self-demeaning frustration and shame.

He had never felt closer to suicide.

---

1. Cynthia Smythe was the only female locomotive driver in England at the time. She and Fabian had a brief affair, which ended when she left him for a Scotsman. This was likely due to a square aspect between Venus and Saturn in his chart, which implies disappointment or incompatibility in romantic relationships and a tendency towards a solitary existence. This is reinforced by Venus in Sagittarius and his Ascendant being Sagittarius.

Chapter 36

After she had left the farm Juanita made her way northwards. She did not like her new name. She preferred to think of herself as Atotoztli.

While she was still in New Spain she had led a wild and lonely existence. She avoided people as much as she could. They had already burned her twice as a witch.

Her progress was painfully slow from a modern perspective. She took over three hundred years to reach New York. Admittedly her progress accelerated with the development of the railway. When she became familiar with it she always travelled by train.

Long before the railways existed she made her way through North America on foot. Though she didn't know it, she was following a course that was almost the exact opposite of the Western Expansion, which was yet to start. She was drifting East. During the course of this journey she became fluent in English and French, and acquired some German and Dutch.

In the forests of the Northwest she met Jack. He was a trapper. She had come across him in a clearing. He was surprised by how she had seemed to appear from nowhere.

Over the course of meandering northwards she had come to an innate understanding. The quality she had once attributed to the goddess Ayauhteotl had always been her own, but it was contingent upon the perceptions of other people. There must be someone present to witness an appearance or disappearance. Without observers there would be neither.

This particular quality of hers was rooted in a combination of time, of which she had an unlimited supply, of the metaphorical interpretation of a rudimentary knowledge of alchemy and the expectations of beholders. It was a kind of trickery that involved immanence. At first she had used it instinctively but when she became aware of what she was doing she developed it into a technique.

It was this technique that allowed her to seemingly appear and disappear, to prevent people from recalling her face, and later to make endless amounts of paper money.

She didn't think in terms of technique though, as that word was yet to become current. She might have thought of it as a 'way'.

Modern people quite often make the error of ascribing their own values and beliefs on to ancient people. Modern people, of course, are those alive on the pinnacle of linear time at any given moment, assuming linear time is vertical. They are often not receptive to the idea that modes of thinking might have been quite different in other times and places. The basic shared experience of being human would have stayed the same perhaps but that was the extent of it.

It is a problem to determine what other people are thinking. I have difficulty knowing what I'm thinking myself, and sometimes wonder if there is such a thing as thought. Therefore, I cannot describe her quality.

If I were to try, I would first imagine quiddity not quality. Then I would consider states that are suggested to me by theoretical physics, which flout the laws of an earlier theoretical physics and thus render the general sense of objective reality void.

In such states there is the possibility of things happening without cause. In addition, nothing that appears real is real, being only a symbol of what is truly real, if there is such a thing.

I can give no satisfactory explanation for how Atotoztli was able to appear and disappear like the mist condensing or evaporating over a lagoon, but if I were to consider it as a poem, then the internal logic would be freed from reason. There would be the beauty of metaphor and cadence, where thought is not separate from emotion—an unexpected spaciousness of architecture.

To be honest, I haven't yet bothered to try to understand her mysterious quality.

Jack wasn't used to women. Whenever he had amassed enough pelts, he would go to the fort to sell them and buy supplies. But he saw mostly soldiers there, not women. He would give them news of the Chinooks, whom he had come to know.

Sometimes, in contradiction to his visits to the fort, he would go in the opposite direction. The Chinooks understood his solitude and did not consider him a threat. They would trade and he would give them information about the soldiers in the fort and other news from the East. Occasionally he would provide them with firearms. He'd even taken on some aspects of the way they viewed the world. But the Chinooks were dying from the pox. He had little connection to their women.

When Atotoztli appeared to him as a vision in the air which solidified over the course of a moment and became a woman of rare beauty, he felt shocked as if he was the one being trapped, but then he felt the pull of desire. He believed she had come to give him a message. He was diffident and expectant.

It took him some time to accept that this was not the case and his diffidence slowly reverted to his normal quiet confidence. She had come here because she had come here, and he had just happened to be here too. A chance encounter. There was no more to it than that. By then they were living together in the forest. They were both solitary people. Their relationship was founded on distance at close quarters, not a distance of anger but of recognition and respect.

She stayed with Jack because she was tired of wandering alone but despite his company she was still lonely. Sometimes she teased him by conjuring animals in his traps. Whenever he went to gather them he would discover they were not there. His frustration amused her.

It was easy enough to accomplish as his life revolved around catching creatures. All she had to do was to exploit his experiences and expectations. She was using his own beliefs to create the illusion that tricked him. She found his trapping of animals unattractive. She was used to the cruelty of sacrifice but Jack's activities were devoid of the deeper currents of life and reminded her more of the rapacious greed and self-justification of the Spaniards in Tenochtitlan. That was what inspired her to trick him.

Sometimes he would get angry with her for chuckling at his confusion when the animal he had plainly seen in the trap vanished as he put his hands upon it. On one occasion he struck her across the face, knocking her to the ground. He was a powerful man.

After that, any respect they'd had for each other began to falter. In Jack's case it was replaced by jealousy. Not that there was anyone to be jealous of. He might have been jealous of her immortality, of which he could not have been conscious, only sensing it in her indifference and in his inability to control her. She took it as a weakness in a man who was otherwise strong. Though she had more time than the world itself, she was not inclined to waste any of it on such a weakness.

On his next journey to the fort, he insisted that she accompany him, as she knew he would. She gave him the slip while he was bartering. She would never know that he died from sepsis after wounding himself when he stumbled into one of his own traps, having tried to alleviate his sorrow with whisky.

***

ON THE MORNING OF September 4th, 1876, a man entered The Fifth Avenue Hotel in New York. He approached the counter and enquired about the price of a suite of rooms for a year.

"I am asking on behalf of The Countess Bukuroshe Afordita Fausta Rugova of Illyria. I am her agent. My name is Agron."

The hotel manager quoted him the price but he felt uneasy. Mr. Agron was well dressed in a finely cut morning coat. His collar was impeccably clean and symmetrical. Upon his head, at an angle which could not be considered jaunty—merely a respectable imitation of jauntiness—rested a black top hat. A hint of gold glimmered between his fingers from the pommel of his cane. Despite his well groomed appearance, there was something strange about Mr. Agron but he couldn't determine what it was exactly. It was just an intuition, a feeling. He watched as Mr. Agron withdrew a purse from his coat and set a thousand dollars upon the counter.

"This will, I assume, include meals?"

"Yes, sir." His misgivings were relieved by the money, so crisp and freshly minted. He put it away in the strong box. The strangeness he had initially felt was no doubt due to Mr. Agron's foreign ways. Dignitaries from abroad were a boon to the hotel. He felt a surge of respect for his boss, the owner, Mr. Enos, and his perseverance despite harsh criticism that only a fool would invest his fortune in a northern backwater. How he had proved them wrong! Twenty third Street was the height of fashion these days, and all because of his foresight. This was the finest hotel in the city. He was happy to oblige this distinguished foreign gentleman.

"When will the Countess require her rooms, sir?"

"Tomorrow. My mistress enjoys privacy and does not wish to be bothered by servants."

"Yes, sir. I understand. I will instruct my staff."

"The Countess will wait upon herself. She will not be accompanied by her maid, who has been detained by the plague sweeping across our country at present."

This last statement was uttered just for Mr. Agron's own amusement, though the manager did not know that. He felt suddenly uneasy again. Could it be possible that the Countess was infectious? An epidemic would be disastrous for the hotel, and for him too if he was held responsible. But then the rich always had somewhere to go when the need arose. They were most likely clean. He had accepted their money; to suddenly cancel the reservation would be embarrassing. It would reflect badly on him and there would most likely be ramifications.

Mr Agron took the receipt from the counter.

"Good day to you."

He turned and walked back out onto Fifth Avenue.

***

ATOTOZTLI HAD ANGLICISED HER Spanish name to Joanna. She made this change when she reached the town of Intercourse, Pennsylvania. She changed in other ways too over the fourteen years she was there.

She had arrived in the evening and needed somewhere to stay. She didn't want to sleep rough in the fields as the nights were getting cold. Walking down Poplar Street she saw a building that looked like an inn and went inside. She had no money but trusted her powers of persuasion.

The door opened into a large room that looked like a saloon. There were a few women, and some children running around. One of the women came to greet her. She was older than the others and seemed to be the age mortals looked if they reached fifty. She said her name was Grace. Atotoztli introduced herself as Joanna. It was the first time she had used that name. Grace was warm and friendly, she led Joanna to a bathroom with a wash basin and jug of water and waited while she cleaned herself up, then she took her to the kitchen and gave her a bowl of soup.

Grace ran her experienced eye over the newcomer. Her dishevelled and impecunious state and lack of luggage suggested a hasty and unplanned departure—from an unhappy marriage perhaps. She was a little older than most of the girls but after cleaning up from the road, looked remarkably healthy—with lustrous black hair, and pure, bright eyes. Her complexion was good, her skin taut and unblemished. She had an understated exotic beauty.

After breakfast the next morning at the big kitchen table, Grace took Joanna aside.

"I have a proposition for you, my dear. Should you find yourself between commitments you might like to stay with us a while and work for your keep."

Joanna thought for a moment in silence.

"What would you have me do?"

Grace wondered at the naïveté of this woman, who otherwise seemed so intelligent. She was feigning ignorance perhaps, clinging to a vestige of morality.

"We entertain gentlemen, my dear, six days a week. We refrain on Sundays, it being the Lord's day."

Atotoztli had never considered prostitution as a way to pass her time. But why not? Raw sexual encounters with mortals would be an education. She did not seek connection. She would always remain detached but she craved comfort, something she had experienced when she was young on account of her noble birth. The last few centuries had been notably lacking in that regard and she began to see possibilities for herself that would benefit from a more visceral understanding of the mortals around her.

Grace kept talking.

"I keep a good house. My girls are well cared for. We are like a big family here. You'll be able to make some good money before you choose to move on. What do you think?"

"When do I start?"

This caught Grace off guard. She had not expected such a quick and easy acquiescence. Joanna had no doubt done this before and was pretending to be ignorant for some reason of her own. She was an odd one.

She glanced at a young boy playing with a spinning top. "Tonight then, my dear. I can instruct you in ways to avert accidents, should you wish."

"No need. I am... how do you say it... barren?"

"I'll pay you seventy-five cents an encounter. You'll stand to earn thirteen or fourteen dollars a week. That's good money. From that I'll deduct your room and board, and some money from your first week's pay to cover the clothing I'll provide you. Pay day is Sunday, The Lord's day." She smiled and rose from her chair.

Clients generally arrived in the evening. The ladies would greet them in the lounge, engage them in conversation and serve them expensive drinks. They would baulk at the price but always paid it. Grace kept an eye on things. She had a shotgun behind the bar. The gentlemen would make their selection, or selections, and would be led upstairs to the rooms assigned for the purpose.

There were many repeat customers who had their favourites, and Joanna's presence altered the dynamic. Little did anyone know how different things would become.

And so she began her work at 'the hotel', as it was euphemistically called. She had sex with mortals two or three times a day, six days a week. She soon developed a glowing reputation.

Her first client—she learned from the other women as he declined to give his name, was the Reverend Amos Fitch, a vicar. He surprised her by lying fully clothed on the bed and requesting that she strip naked and sit in the chair opposite him. He then demanded that she pleasure herself while all the time excoriating her for sin and error. It was not a pleasant experience. He did leave her a bible which turned out to be useful. She worked through it over the following weeks in an attempt to satisfy her curiosity about the beliefs of the conquerors, something that had never interested her before.

Aside from bequeathing her eternal life, Guillermo had taught her how to read. She had learned quickly, but had never read much, being bereft of books. The Bible changed that. It did not bring her any closer to the understanding she desired but it inspired her to read more.

She was helped in that regard by another man who became a regular client of hers—John Osbourne Lecky. He was the private tutor to two children of a wealthy landowner, who also frequented the hotel. Mr. Lecky was a quiet and earnest man of gentle disposition. His demands on her were not unreasonable, though ardent. He quickly fell in love with her. He was a classicist by training and when he noticed her interest he spoke enthusiastically of Ancient Greece and Rome, of Homer and Troy, of the myths and the gods. He recited poems to her in Latin.

His enthusiasm was enhanced by a feeling of contentment unlike anything he could remember.

This was because she had not only given him physical pleasure but had also abstracted it to a different realm, more cerebral and emotionally profound. He felt unified.

She was changing. Though she had lived with mortals for centuries, she had always tried to hide from them, at least since Fabián had died. Now, she no longer felt the need to hide. With that acknowledgement came a sense of purpose, and unconsciously at first she honed her abilities. At a whim she could now control a mortal's emotional state.

She was going to do whatever she wanted and she would do it in comfort.

Mr. Lecky brought books for her on his frequent visits. He introduced her to Voltaire and Shakespeare. He gave her books on philosophy and mathematics. He gave her poetry. She devoured them all. No matter how much she read, she wanted more. He told her about the town library and suggested she go there.

Later, she began to dress as a man and walk around the town. She was good at disguise. People saw what they wanted to see. She just helped them along. She visited the library and went back there often.

At meals around the big farmhouse table there was always a lot of laughter about foibles and perversions. There was scorn too. The Sheriff was often discussed. He only lasted two or three minutes, sometimes less. He had no favourites. Any of them would do. Maybe he thought variety would produce a different result. He blamed his own shortcomings on anybody but himself.

When the Sheriff chose Joanna one night, she knew what to expect. Her immortal's sense of time allowed her to make a moment last as long as she wanted, or appear to. In this way she made the Sheriff think he'd lasted for twenty minutes. He left the hotel in a magnanimous mood. The other women wanted to know how she'd done it.

Over the years Grace's health began to fail and she left the day-to-day running of the hotel to Joanna, who had become invaluable—always level headed, responsible, and with an almost magical way of satisfying the customers. Business had never been better. Joanna was her natural successor. Everyone knew it.

And so after Grace died she took over. She stopped taking clients, except for rare occasions, and then only very selectively. She denied the Sheriff repeatedly. He reminded her of Alvarado—a violent man who cared only for himself. One of the first things she did was to raise the women's pay. She increased the price for customers too, who grumbled but did not stop coming. They were experiencing the hotel in a different way. It was no longer just a brothel but a mysterious paradise. They left satiated and enhanced in spirit. Their memories were dreams, their lives transformed.

She used a kind of mass hypnosis to affect the moods of all the occupants, both clients and staff, filling them with hallucinatory pleasures that came in waves and withdrew leaving contentment.

By this time she had devised her system for creating money from newspapers. As with her other abilities it was nebulous and would have seemed like magic to mortals. For her it was just a process, but if magic was a general term to describe the wilful manipulation of forces that could not be explained rationally, then it would be a good enough word to describe what she was doing.

She was going to become extremely wealthy. It was not personal gain that inspired her. Riches were the means by which she could implement her idea from so many years ago. Wealth was the vessel she would embark upon to navigate the river of greed which flowed through the mortals around her. Their printed word would be the medium. She chose to use it because the stories were analogous to the civilisation that had told them. Guillermo had shown her the power of analogy.

As an experiment and to amuse herself, she left the hotel one day dressed as a man and hid stacks of money in places where they would be soon found, taking care not to be observed. Each stack was five hundred dollars—a year's wages for the average person. She was curious to see what would happen.

The money was found. Some people put it in banks, others locked it in boxes beneath their beds.

A clandestine elation flowed into her mind.

Then the money ceased to exist. This was an intermittent problem when she first started making money. Occasionally it would suddenly disappear but not always. She had no explanation for it. After further experimentation she was able to make money that lasted.

The disappearance went unnoticed in the banks but those with strongboxes soon discovered their loss. They believed they had been robbed. Suspicions spread, friendships were sundered, marriages marred by violence, old enmities rekindled. She had sewn discord.

Many years later her tampering with financial markets would cause a global depression. This would be revenge, but without vindictiveness, and afterwards her need for vengeance would be satisfied.

She left the hotel when it started to bore her and when her employees became older than she was.

She was more like a goddess then, than she had ever been before but it no longer concerned her. Everyone becomes herself, she thought.

CHAPTER 37

On September 5th, 1876, as arranged, the Countess Bukuroshe Afordita Fausta Rugova arrived at The Fifth Avenue Hotel. The bellboys and porters sprang into action when her carriage pulled up outside. They whisked her trunks into the lobby and up to her suite.

The manager came out to greet her. The Countess was alone, which he found unusual. People of her standing normally came with a retinue. He had been expecting to see Mr. Agron at least but he had learned to suppress his own curiosity. The privacy of a guest was paramount. Gossip was inevitable in a hotel such as this and he was quick to admonish the staff when he caught them at it. He was a stickler for discipline and self control.

He was relieved that the Countess appeared to be in perfect health. She was sumptuously dressed, as befitted a woman of her rank, attractive but not showy or pretentious. She acknowledged his welcome with a smile but no words. It was likely, he thought, that she was not familiar with the English language. He would not burden her with prolonged conversation. He instructed a bellboy to take her up to her suite.

As he watched her drift elegantly across the lobby he felt satisfied with his work. It was a small affirmation of the part he played in the beautiful order of the world. He remained in good spirits for the rest of the day.

A few hours later he looked up from his ledger to see Mr. Agron again.

"Welcome back, sir. I trust the Countess is comfortable. I have given orders that her privacy is to be respected."

"Thank you. The Countess is satisfied with her accommodations. She has asked for newspapers."

"Yes of course, sir."

"The titles she requires are: *The New-York Tribune, The Sun, The New York Times, The New York Evening Post, The Daily Standard, The New Yorker Staats-Zeitung, The Brooklyn Daily Eagle, The Daily Graphic* and *The New York World.* These should be delivered every day and left outside her door. The following journals should be delivered weekly—*The New York Ledger, The Sunday Mercury,* and *The New York Sunday News.*"

The manager had to resort to pen and paper.

"Will that be all, sir?"

"Yes. That will suffice at present."

The Countess had by this time unpacked her trunks and put everything away. She sat on an armchair and filled her pipe, gazing down at Fifth Avenue. She had made the right decision coming to this hotel. She had heard it was the best and most luxurious in the city. It seemed to have been built in such a way that the rooms were insulated from external sounds, not that she was especially bothered by sound but it was pleasing nonetheless.

Having seen the effect of leaving money around in Intercourse, she intended to continue in the same vein but on a grander scale. She would disrupt what they called the economy. This city was a good place to do it.

Her vengeance began to form. It sought balance, not punishment out of anger. She would leave large amounts of money in areas where it would likely be discovered by the impoverished. The wealthy would believe they were threatened by the masses. Confidence would fail, confusion would abound. This would set the balance.

She was going to make a lot of money and soon she would have the raw material she needed.

She had enjoyed being Agron, ordering the newspapers and booking the suite. After she left Intercourse, she had travelled mostly as a man. She found that when she was a man she felt like a man. To test her disguise she had taken to hiring prostitutes. So effective was her magic that none of them suspected her. She was falling under the spell of her own illusion and began experimenting with what it was like to be a dog, or a bird, or a cat.

Over the next few months she busied herself making money, ensconced in her suite, bothered by no one. She stored the stacks of banknotes in her empty trunks. She broke her routine by slipping out and roaming the city, exploring the different areas and seeing where best to make her disbursements. Occasionally she would go down to the dining room to take her meals, and to observe the other guests. She also thought it was a good idea to show herself from time to time to avoid knocks on the door and questions about her well-being.

On several occasions, a man dining alone had caught her eye. He was old for a mortal and was probably nearing the end of his life. She liked the way he looked—intelligent and kind. After creating so much wealth alone in her suite, she wanted to speak to someone. Solitary diners either kept their heads down, embarrassed by their loneliness, or they looked around them in search of company to assuage it. She could see he was of the latter sort, and was studying her when he thought she wasn't looking.

When he finished his meal he passed by her table. She made use of the opportunity by allowing her napkin to fall. He stooped to pick it up and placed it on the table.

"Dr John Gray. Glad to be of service, Madam."

"Thank you Doctor. I am Countess Bukuroshe Afordita Fausta Rugova, and am honoured to make your acquaintance."

"My apologies, Countess. Please forgive an old man his errors. Good day."

After that they would greet each other if they met in the dining room or lobby. Several weeks later, Dr Gray suggested they take coffee together.

The Countess drew him out with her questions.

He told her of his medical career, and how, though sceptical at first he had become convinced of homoeopathy. It had been his life's work. That was not to say it should exclude allopathy. They could coexist quite happily.

"But that is all in the past now. It has been almost ten years since I lost my beloved wife, Elizabeth. Our children have grown. And so I sold my house and came to live here, at The Fifth Avenue

Hotel. I cannot say I regret it. But I fear I have monopolised the conversation, Countess. Pray tell me of yourself, if it is not impolite of me to ask. From where do you hail?"

Unlike most of the people she had encountered, the Countess was not in the habit of talking about herself. She was more interested in learning about the lives of these mortals, especially since she had embarked upon her economic adventure.

"I fear my life would appear tawdry to a man who has made so many contributions to society. The lottery of birth has afforded me a leisurely existence. I am a widow and I manage my estates in Illyria. I am touring your country to satisfy my indolent curiosity and also to look out for promising investments. This great city is the place of the future."

A flicker of puzzlement crossed the old man's face.

"I am saddened to hear you have been widowed so young, Countess. I am old and have not kept abreast of foreign affairs, so please correct me if I'm wrong but what I know of Illyria is that it was an ancient country, or collection of city states that was absorbed into the Roman Empire some two thousand years ago and no longer exists today. But perhaps the name is still used locally?"

She had learned of Illyria from a book John Lecky had given her and had assumed it was still in existence. Dr Gray had caught her out. Up until now she had wanted to listen to him talk about his life without manipulating him in any way, but should he discuss her with others her position would become awkward and she would have to move on. She liked The Fifth Avenue Hotel and did not want to leave it yet. Dr Gray had an honesty and humbleness about him. He reminded her a little of Fabián—the only man she had ever loved, or came close to loving. She didn't wish to hurt him. She would have to hint at the truth without telling it, to demonstrate without explanation.

The Countess suddenly disappeared, leaving Dr Gray alone with his coffee cup.

She saw the shock on his face as he sat and looked around him. Then he got up and made his way to his room. She followed and slipped through the door behind him. She waited while he took off his jacket and loosened his collar and then she reappeared.

The doctor was agitated and collapsed into a chair.

"Countess...are you...are you from the spirit world?"

She smiled at him and used her mind to calm him.

"What is it you wish for, Doctor?"

"I long for my wife, Elizabeth. I have taken to Spiritualism, Countess, in the hope that I might commune with her once more. I have attended many séances but all in vain. I fear that only death will join us."

"Lie down on your bed, Doctor, and close your eyes. Wait a while longer and I will bring her to you."

When he opened his eyes, his wife was lying beside him. She cupped his cheeks with her hands.

"Oh John, how I have missed you."

They embraced and made love.

Then he fell into a peaceful sleep.

Chapter 38

Mercury in the First House and Mars in the Ninth, along with Sagittarius as his Ascendant might have influenced Fabian's decision to follow the route taken by Xenophon in the March of the Ten Thousand. He wanted to do it on foot like those ancient hoplites but he estimated the journey was about three thousand miles and with the condition of his leg it just wasn't feasible. He would have to settle for the combustion engine and walk short distances when he was able.

Those two planets in their respective houses can also apparently indicate a certain restlessness and a tendency towards obsessiveness, which might explain his desire to retrace the route for no particular reason other than to accomplish it, as well as his preoccupation with the Russian doll effect and his feeling of being somehow irrelevant to himself.

He missed Gruff. He had left her with Helen and hadn't picked her up since he got back from Mexico. It was a better life for a dog there, and she had become a fixture of the household. She was an old dog now. It was probably for the best and left him free of responsibility. But he still missed that particular relationship he'd had with her.

He started his journey in Kuşadasi, on the Aegean coast in Turkey, which at the time of Xenophon was called Pygela and was near Ephesus in Ionia from where The Ten Thousand had set out. The chances were that there had never actually been exactly ten thousand. Who could say? It was a nice number, though.

When he went to Mexico he'd had a goal in mind, even if he was not certain what it was. On this trip the route of The Ten Thousand would be just an itinerary from which he could deviate whenever he wanted to, or when chance decreed it. He expected to be away for a few months. He saw it as a holiday from himself.

Fabian was excited to finally arrive in Baghdad. It was in this vicinity that the fateful battle of Cunaxa had taken place. It was where Cyrus the Younger was killed leading a cavalry charge against the army of his older brother, Artaxerxes II, leaving the Ten Thousand without an employer or a purpose.

Not long after the burglary, Fabian had visited Dr French and suggested that he should do another LSD session. French was acting strangely, not at all like himself. He barely remained seated and kept pacing over to the window and looking down into the street. He seemed very distracted and anxious. The seven minutes they spent together felt like an hour. Then on one of his ambulations French went to his desk and took the pill bottle from the drawer. He shook out two Delysid tablets into Fabian's palm.

"You can do it on your own this time," he said.

Now that he had arrived in Baghdad, Fabian intended to take one of them when he visited the site of the battlefield at Cunaxa.

He thought the drug would help him uncover the memories hidden in the landscape. The idea that the environment was a repository of memory was inspired by his growing interest in Barianism.

A few days before leaving London he had been browsing in a book shop near the British Museum. He wanted to buy a copy of Xenophon's *Anabasis* to read on the trip. While looking for it, he came across a book entitled *The Annotated Whereto Fore* that aroused his interest. In the foreword he learned that this was an annotated version of the book *Whereto Fore*[1] by the Lebanese Swedish poet Gustavus Namoor, who had written it in Paris while under siege in the Franco-Prussian war and had paid to have it published in London when he moved there soon after.

Whereto Fore was a long poem that sometimes veered into prose, interspersed with a succession of quatrains. It was a discourse between Barian and his disciples. Barian was a kind of prophet and his rambling opinions created powerful images and unexpected juxtapositions. The book was unsuccessful at the time but was rediscovered by Stefana Stevens in 1904 and was republished by Chapman and Hall in 1906. It became a source of inspiration for the artists and occultists at the time. They saw *Whereto Fore* as a guide to a new aesthetic which they called Barianism. It took the

---

1. *Whereto Fore* was derided by the few critics who bothered to read it. They considered it an empty expression of the lassitude of the Eastern mind and pure humbug. One of them, the humorist Charles Edward Morel, claimed that his brain was bigger than Namoor's. Namoor sued Morel for libel. The judge, stating that both men's brains would have to be removed to determine the veracity of the claim, threw the case out of court.

form of a pseudo-religious belief system. Barian was both fool and sage.

The Annotated Whereto Fore started life as a monthly literary journal. Each issue included a section of the poem, along with comments and interpretations of the text from multiple contributors. When the whole poem had been treated in this way, the journal was discontinued. In 1910 Gordon Alladyce, the playwright, took it upon himself to assemble all the issues into a book. He dramatised selected comments, merging them with the original discourse of the poem, and so Barianism became a fully fledged idea.

Gustavus Namoor was appalled by what he considered such an obscene interpretation of his poem. He refused to ever speak of it again, and slipped back into the obscurity from which he had arisen.

Fabian stood by the bookshelf and read the entire foreword. He was immediately taken by it. *The Annotated Whereto Fore* and *Anabasis* were the only two books he brought with him on his journey.

The semi-sextile between Neptune and Jupiter in his chart would have made Fabian more susceptible to such ideas as Barianism, as it denoted a tendency towards mysticism and spiritual concerns.

He studied the shape the route of The Ten Thousand created on the map. Cunaxa was its easternmost extremity. It was the point of transition where advance became retreat. Afterwards the line wandered off along the coast of The Black Sea. Barianism recognised the importance of extremities. It was at such points that geographical memories were most potent, transcending the merely human and expressing pure reality, beyond the reach of comprehension. There were other extremities to the place too—not so much physical as metaphorical—such as the death of Cyrus, which extinguished certain histories while fostering others. Geographical memory extended beyond the planet Earth and was part of the structure of the ever changing Universe, which was in a perpetual state of creation.

Looking at the map again, he realised that this was the Knight's Tour that Dr French had mentioned, and he was about to complete the last square. Taking a dose of LSD at the site of the battlefield would facilitate his perception of the landscape and its memories. It would be a short cut—a short cut to eternity. He hoped he would be rid forever of his obsessive tendency to imagine things inside other things.

There was a problem, however. The exact location of Cunaxa was unknown. It was on the banks of the Euphrates but there were differing opinions as to where.

This was a disappointment. He spent the next week sightseeing in Baghdad. Each day he would venture from his hotel with only one place in mind to visit. In this way he would not overload himself and fully appreciate what he saw. He would be able to enjoy the unexpected on his way there and back.

On his visit to the bazaar one day, he had an unpleasant surprise when Burnham called out and approached him from across the street.

"What are you doing here?"

"I'm here because you are, my son."

Fabian was angry. He'd always intended to confront Burnham about the theft if he ever encountered him again. He hadn't expected to meet him in Baghdad. It threw him off.

"What do you mean? And don't call me 'my son'. You're the last person I'd want as a father."

"Testy, aren't we? I'm following you. It's my job. Why the fuck did you have to come all the way to Baghdad? I'm not getting paid enough for this."

"All you think about is money. Is that why you stole my book?"

"I didn't steal nothing from you."

"Oh no? And by the way, 'anything' is the word, not 'nothing'. I had the book on my desk when you were in my flat. I saw you looking at it. I know what you're about."

"You don't know nothing, mate."

"So why did you steal it?"

"I didn't steal it. I took it."

"You took it? What's the difference?"

"The difference is I returned it to its rightful owner. You're the one who stole it. Off that woman on a train. I've heard your story. I've seen the manuscript. Yes, there's a manuscript about you."

Fabian stalled. Burnham was right. He had stolen it. He had no idea what manuscript he was talking about.

"So who's the rightful owner?"

"Can't tell you that."

"Well if you've returned the book, why are you still following me?"

"Because it's still my job."

"Who are you working for?"

"I can't say. The Official Secrets act, mate. They've got me by the balls, see? But I'll tell you what, my son, seeing as we go back. There is people what think you're a spy. One of those communists working for the Russians."

"That's nonsense. I'm on holiday."

"Well, it don't look so good you coming out here on your tod, does it? Why d'you come here anyway?"

"I'm retracing the route taken by Xenophon and The Ten Thousand."

"Who the fuck is Xenophon?"

Chapter 39

After she had brought him his wife, Dr Gray kept wanting to see her, again and again. She humoured him a few times. He was vigorous for an old mortal. She hadn't intended to make it a permanent arrangement but she had come to see how much he loved his wife. She had never met a man who loved his wife so much. Either that, or he was what they called a 'player'—but a good one. She decided to keep bringing him his wife until he died. Then she would leave the hotel. She cared for him in a way that she hadn't for any mortal since Fabiàn and it made her feel good.

Agron, or her new American agent, Robert Cummings, had to extend her yearly rental a number of times. The manager had been replaced by another, who was just as polite but more combative in a subtle way. He had a thinly veiled curiosity about the Countess that she didn't like.

Dr Gray often asked her to accompany him to spiritualist meetings. Perhaps he wanted to show her off. She was prepared to give him pleasure and the means with which to take it, but she would not be surrounded by mortals who would like to assume they knew her.

Dr Gray died in 1882. She imagined him meeting his wife again as unlikely as it was. Death was a big place. By the time he died he had known it was not Elizabeth she was bringing to him but herself, though he kept up the pretence.

She left The Fifth Avenue Hotel soon after. Luxury and comfort were beginning to bore her. Floating on their river of greed had become commonplace and was no longer satisfying. She had made enough money to last for years and had sent Cummings to open a bank account for her in his name. There would be money available when she needed it and she could enjoy some respite from forgery. The Countess would not be seen again.

Joanna Sprague took a room at the St Stephen Hotel in Greenwich Village in the summer of 1882. She had a husband called William, though they were never there at the same time together. It was a novel idea that had not occurred to her before—for one person to be a married couple. She found it amusing and enjoyed it when one or the other of them went out and befriended interesting looking mortals.

After her staid existence in comfort and luxury, she had decided to lead a more colourful life. It had taken Fabiàn's death for her to leave the farm and Dr Gray's for her to leave the hotel. She was concerned that her actions were contingent on those of mortals. Even her habit of leaving large amounts of money lying around fit into that mould, because she did it to gain a reaction from them. Deep within herself she felt it should be the other way round. Perhaps she should remove herself completely from the power struggles between gods and men. She would never be able to do as she wanted if she was beholden to someone else's idea.

This inspired her to live on the street as a cat for a while. She enjoyed the immediacy and lack of pretence being a cat, though the latent cruelty and ignorance of humans was still apparent.

She resumed her human form and continued to stay at St Stephen Hotel with William, who was not there when she was. A perfect situation.

She would sometimes see a woman standing on the corner playing a flute—her beautiful plaintive melody finding its way through the sounds of horse carts and conversations, and filling the street. A man she met told her about a book he had written using every word ever spoken. He interested her until he began following her around, always present at the places she frequented. William took up with a wealthy patroness of the arts who was soon smitten with him. She generally preferred the women to the men.

She spent the next fifty or sixty years exploring Manhattan.

Chapter 40

He had almost given up the hope that this day would ever come, and then it had arrived from nowhere. Whenever he had needed help from criminals he had always given them a description of his book just in case they should come across it. This time the big thug had finally proved his worth, even though he'd been cagey about its provenance.

He sat back in his chair, holding the book with both hands. Then slowly he thumbed through the pages, recognising his faded script, resting his eyes upon it, and remembering when he had written it. His excitement and fascination were the same as when he had first begun studying the Art.

He set the book on his desk. He would soon be free. Already he could feel release. He would decipher it using his key, recording the results on his notepad. He paused a moment to savour the expectation, then he took up his fountain pen.

But he could make no sense of what he had written. The key didn't work.

His first thought was that this was not his book. This was not what he had written at all. His excitement was becoming desperation. He examined it closely, studying every page, the paper, the script, the binding. It was definitely his book. It had aged naturally enough but its familiarity still called out to him.

Was it possible that he had forgotten the key? It was highly unlikely. He had created a mnemonic —three images he imagined, which aided his memory. He had run through them everyday since he had first encoded it. He had not forgotten.

Then the code itself must have changed. But it looked just the same as it ever had, so the change would have to be in the relationship between the code and the key—the way they communicated. It might have something to do with information theory and about loss in transmission, or degradation of meaning.

Their relationship was unique. They were entangled. What affected one would affect the other. And now they had both mutated. The key he remembered was worthless.

Whatever had been bad before was now worse.

He needed to go outside. He left the building and walked along St Marks Crescent and turned left into Regents Park Road. He had no destination in mind and no purpose other than to keep moving. As he walked he let the mnemonic run through his mind. He saw the reflection of arches in the clear water of the pool at the Alhambra. Then he looked at the arches themselves and counted them. They gave him the number seven. The beauty of the place calmed him. He conjured the second image—Huēyi Teōcalli, the two temples, the Hill of Sustenance, and the Hill of Coatepec. The number two.

Before he began to picture the third image in the sequence, he glanced up. On a corner by Gloucester Avenue was a woman. She was standing, looking around her, taking her bearings, as if lost. She had an ethereal beauty and an aura of calm detachment. He had only seen that combination in one person. He felt as if awakened from enchanted slumber, suddenly alive, infused with love. Juanita. It couldn't be.

He called out her name and ran across the street without waiting for a response.

"Oi! Watch out, you idiot!"

It was the rag and bone man. He narrowly avoided being run down by his horse. The cart clattered off down the street. She was still on the corner.

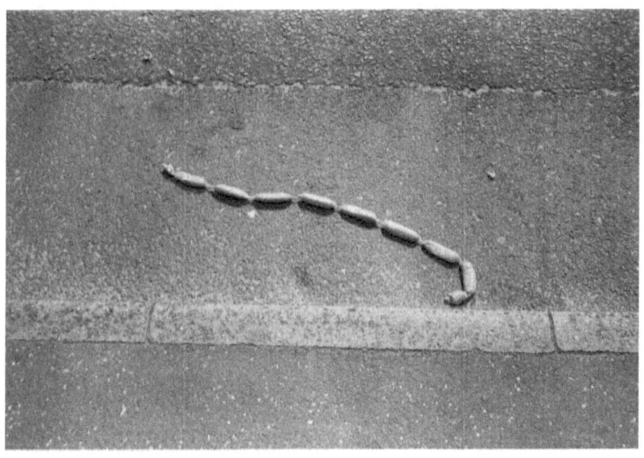

"Juanita?"

There was no recognition in her eyes.

"*Soy yo, Guillermo.*"

She had forgotten him. He spoke to her in Nahuatl.

"*Ax tijmati ajkia na?*"

She had the coldness and polite disdain of a woman receiving unwanted attention and looking for a way out. She turned abruptly and walked off down Gloucester Avenue.

Even though he was eight hundred and forty years old, this was too much for one day. To have found what he most desired—what he had desired for so many mortal lifetimes, and then to have it taken from him moments later was an irony so cruel he could not bear it. He had found his book and lost it. He could not let the same thing happen with Juanita. She was half way down the street and walking fast.

He followed her.

CHAPTER 41

YOU ARE INVITED TO attend a lecture by Dr Lawrence Shadwell upon the subject of existence.

221 Baker Street, London NW1 at 1:00 pm on Sunday December 7th 1958. This lecture will be held in the basement of the building and is free of charge. Refreshments will be provided.

It looked like a hoax, or a confidence trick. A lecture in a basement? No admission fee? There was no information about the lecturer, no list of credentials. What could they possibly be after? He studied the envelope for a clue. It was innocuous enough—less rectangular and slightly larger than normal, hand-written, beige in colour. The post mark was illegible.

He slipped the invitation back into its envelope with the intention of throwing it away but something stayed his hand. He placed it on the mantelpiece instead, from where it watched him as he moved about the room.

On the appointed day Fabian walked down the steps to the basement at 221 Baker Street, one hand on the rail, the other on his cane, step after careful step. It was a cold and sunny day and he had come by foot from his flat in Manchester Square.

His leg had been getting worse over the years. He ought to do something about it but he hated going to see doctors. That accident at Durdle Door didn't seem so fortunate now. Though if he hadn't been injured, he might have died like so many others, but still, walking with a stick at the age of thirty-eight seemed a cruel act of fate. He could remember the strange bird soaring above him, the muffled sound of the waves. The terrible pain. It could have been yesterday, or tomorrow. Just not today.

He passed through a foyer into a large room. The ceilings were low and the lighting soft. He was expecting something seedier. There was a makeshift stage, skirted in black satin, with chairs arranged before it in neat rows and a lectern upon it. Quite a few people were milling about. The floors were carpeted. The walls were white, gilded by the warm light. The place felt elegant and comfortable but it had a labyrinthine quality.

Fabian wandered around, looking for the gents. Smaller rooms and nooks opened off the main area. In one of them was a bar. Above it was a sign that had recently been added, hand-written and slightly off kilter, which said 'Refreshments'. The counter was empty. It struck him as odd that he hadn't seen any staff at all and the mysterious Dr Shadwell was nowhere in evidence.

He found the facilities because they were the only rooms with doors, aside from the kitchen. They were marked with the astrological symbols for Mars and Venus.

He rested his cane against the wall next to the urinal. Moments later someone else came in and a familiar voice rang out.

"What do we have here then? A leprechaun, is it?"

Burnham was looking down over the divider at him with a big grin and that glimmer of kindness in his eyes, so incongruous with the rest of his character.

Fabian smiled back up at him. "Bugger off, Burnham. Let a man piss in peace." Then he finished as quickly as he could, snatched up his cane and got out before he was engaged in conversation.

He saw Helen by the empty refreshment counter. She seemed flustered.

"Do you know that during the week this place operates as a restaurant where businessmen have their lunch served to them by women dressed as schoolgirls?"

It was just like Helen to check on where she was going. "There's something wrong about this whole thing."

"Why did you come, then?"

"Because it intrigued me."

They went back into the main room, which was now quite full, and found two empty seats in the front row. It was almost one o'clock, time for the lecture to begin but there was still no sign of Shadwell. Fabian wondered if he was ever going to appear and whether this event would just turn out to be an elaborate prank.

His doubts were allayed when a man in a black suit with a narrow tie and thick tortoiseshell glasses came out of nowhere and stepped on to the stage. He carried a sheaf of papers which he set on the lectern.

"Good afternoon ladies and gentlemen. Thank you all so much for coming. I'm Dr Lawrence Shadwell. The subject of my...."

He was interrupted by a sudden commotion. Fabian turned to see that Zlodyk had come into the room with a cohort of followers. He was a charismatic figure, in full Turkish regalia. Fabian had never seen him before but it couldn't be anyone else. Helen had turned to look as well.

"What a character.... Oh look, there's Dr French."

Fabian followed her gaze. French was sitting with a very beautiful woman. It was funny to see him outside his consulting room. It felt like spying. Then he did a double take—French's companion—she was the woman he had seen on the train and in the hotel in Mexico City, whose book he had taken. He was sure of it.

Shadwell waited for the room to settle, then he continued.

"The subject of my talk today is existence. Before I begin, I should like to say that all of you were personally invited, and for one reason alone—you all share a common trait. 'We are all people,' you might say, and you would be right. But the trait I refer to is more specific and I shall get to it shortly."

He was a good speaker, polished and confident. He was able to project his voice without the use of a microphone and without needing to shout. His pacing and intonation were excellent. He must have had years of experience lecturing students and was most probably a university professor.

Fabian felt reassured. This might not be so bad after all.

"Existence—the state of being real. But what actually is it? That's a question that has concerned philosophers since ancient times and still does.

"Let me give you a brief overview. The discipline in philosophy which examines this question is known as ontology. As might be expected there are different opinions. For our purposes today, these differences could essentially be divided into two categories—that of the second-order property, or property of properties, and that of the first-order property, or property of individuals.

"Of course there are further distinctions—singular and general, physical and mental, concrete and abstract, possible and necessary. But can there be different degrees of existence? And why should anything exist at all?"

A loud snoring was coming from the back of the room. Fabian turned again to see Burnham slouched over on his chair. Someone must have nudged him because there was a snort and then the snoring ceased. Shadwell chuckled.

"Well at least I'm holding your attention so far. Maybe I should cut to the chase. Now when I said that you all shared a common trait, I was referring to the fact that in a general sense none of you exist."

He was met with a stony silence.

"To elaborate—what you perceive as your existence is the product of an author. Now let me be quite clear, I am not using this word metaphorically. I am not implying that you were created by God. What I'm referring to here is a particular author of the fleshly variety. Your presence here today is the result of being written about. How do I know this? Because I have read his books."

There was movement in the room—murmuring, coughing and the shuffling of feet.

"Don't get me wrong. This is no cause for alarm. The argument of the first-order property allows for Being without Existence. Meinong states that some entities do not exist and therefore object-hood is independent from existence. You can safely regard yourselves as non-existent objects and still retain the state of being.

"I can understand if you don't believe me but you can easily see for yourselves. There is a simple test you can administer, a little subjective perhaps but valid nonetheless. Examine your lives and memories. Look for gaps—paying attention to any that are wider than you would normally expect. For example, what do you remember of your parents, or siblings? What was their hair colour? Can you remember your childhood?

"You see, the characters in a book usually take second place to what the author wishes to do with them, so the author will concentrate on details that are pertinent to the story. Much will be omitted. It might be for the sake of style, expediency or just a paucity of imagination, or even laziness perhaps. For you this means gaps in your lives. So examine yourselves."

Fabian noticed that Helen had clasped his hand. He thought of his parents—a strict and distant father, a remote and disinterested mother. Hair colour? He had black hair, so the chances were they'd had the same. What were their names? Could they have been Arthur and Virginia? He wasn't sure. There were no specific childhood memories he could recall except linoleum. He remembered going to school but not exactly what had happened there. It was disturbing. To be denied the existence which he had taken for granted felt like being robbed, as when Burnham had broken into his flat and stolen the book. But how could he be certain that there had ever been a book? Of course, it could all be nonsense.

Shadwell surveyed his audience for a moment, as if to gauge the effect of his words.

"Now the reason I'm telling you this, is...."

Zlodyk had risen from his chair. The attention in the room was instantly drawn to him as light into a black hole.

"And vegetables?"

Shadwell looked nonplussed, "Vegetables? What about them?"

"Are they written by author, or just eaten?"

"Written? Well, yes…. In many cases…. I would suppose so. An interesting question."

"What you postulate, sir, makes not a jot of differences. Your sadistic invitation to dungeon create wastage of times."

This was pure Zlodyk, his English fluent enough but imperfect, marred by erroneous grammar and an unusual choice of words, slightly archaic in effect. Perhaps this was deliberate. Either way, his imperfection seemed to ennoble him. He was a towering presence.

Already tall, his incredible Janissary's helmet gave him another foot or two. It was a bronze-looking pillbox that sprouted a huge fan-like plumage of white feathers emanating from a silver tube on the right side, and a lone black feather on the left. Between them was coiled a turban of white linen that spilled down his back to below his shoulders. Fabian wondered why he dressed in such an outlandish style.

Janissaries had originally been slaves, taken from their Christian parents and brought up to guard the sultan, their surrogate father, bound forever to his service. There was no one else he could trust. It was standard practice when a new sultan came to power to have his brothers murdered—something that would surely turn them against him. This was the paranoia of absolute monarchy. The Janissaries eventually evolved into a formidable independent force. Zlodyk was canny. He was aware of the symbolism. It gave him the ability, as a powerless, homeless man to imprison the sultan and reduce him to a puppet.

Shadwell's confidence and oratorical abilities were no match. He'd had the rug pulled out from underneath him. He stood in awkward silence.

Zlodyk strode from the room, turning to walk backwards through the doorway, and bowing as he did so to avoid brushing his feathers against the lintel. His entourage hurried after him.

The room burst into a sudden hubbub as the audience all stood up and made for the exit. No one paid any more attention to Shadwell. Only Dr French and his girlfriend remained in their seats.

That instant of chaos stuck in Fabian's mind like a photograph of motion suspended in time—the two anxious men in RAF uniforms, Charlie with his one hand on his chair back, his other empty sleeve dangling at his side, the Mediterranean looking girl, the multitude of faceless people—not that they were actually faceless, it only felt as if they were. He thought he saw the blond, translucent, pale man who had appeared at the foot of his bed so many years ago.

An angry crowd spilled out into Baker Street and into the beautiful winter sunlight—nostalgic and precise, so particular to that latitude. It bathed the city in ancient glory.

The crowd lost its cohesion, breaking first into groups and then to lone individuals, who drifted away in different directions.

Soon it was as if no one had been there at all.

Postscript

Jupiter in the Eighth House bestows a peaceful and easy death. Saturn in the Eighth House portends a long life. Fabian Lear Davis died in his sleep on March 17th, 2004—St Patrick's day. Perhaps only I can see the irony in that. He had just turned eighty-four.

Had certain events in his life been slightly different, he would have been regarded as one of the most unusual and creative film directors of his era, at a time when filmmaking was still considered an art. He would have been in the league of Fellini, Truffaut, Bergman and Ford perhaps, not so much out of the mainstream but above it.

I am to blame. I broke my word. If I had stuck to the horoscope and not interfered with his life he would have been a resounding success. Jupiter in Leo suggests extraordinary public acclaim, particularly in the Arts. Uranus in Aquarius is associated with genius and the tendency to have an impact on a large number of people. The Moon in the First House implies a desire for fame.

So many other details in his chart preordained him for greatness, but I chose to be selective with the material I used. Perhaps it was because I shied away from writing about an important, influential person. I had always intended my subject to be an everyman after all. Fabian was certainly not that, despite his lack of success.

I met him once. It was around 1966 or '67. I would have been eight or nine years old. My mother and Helen had been friends at university, and for some reason they chose to reconnect after not having seen each other for years. Helen came to our house one winter evening and she brought Fabian along. My mother must have known him at university too. He had apparently been living abroad in America for a long time but had come back to England. I remember being struck by his jet black hair and piercing blue eyes. His face seemed to glint with amusement.

While my mother talked to Helen, he spent some time with me. I showed him all my Thunderbirds toys and told him how I wanted Thunderbird Five. It was the big one, the space station. I'd been saving up for it, but it was so expensive. I was hoping my parents would give it to me for Christmas, but they probably wouldn't.

He was interested in what I thought about the world. We talked for a while about respect and what it meant. We talked about philosophy, and the way plastic smelled. We ate grapes. He made me feel very grown-up and wise. I told him that I liked to write and that I'd written a play. I went to get it and handed it to him. It was written on yellow sheets that came from boxes of photographic paper. I realise now that they must have been the separators for the emulsified paper. My sister's boyfriend, who was a photographer, had given them to me. The blank sheets were exciting. They cried out to be covered by words.

Fabian read the whole thing and didn't just pretend to. He told me that it was good and I should keep at it. I would be a great writer one day and who knows what wonderful stories and fantastic characters I would invent?

That Christmas a package arrived for me with Thunderbird Five in it.

The End of The Beginning

Appendices

Appendix 1

Authorial Intrusion

There is a precedent for books in which characters are aware of their author. Sometimes they argue. Flann O'Brien's *At Swim-Two-Birds* comes to mind. There have been earlier books that deal with this issue—*Niebla* by Miguel de Unamuno and *A Sensation Novel* by W.S. Gilbert

In this book the characters are not aware of the author, with the exception of Fabian perhaps, who has inklings but never draws them to any conclusion. Shadwell's lecture is an attempt to make them aware, though it is not completely successful. Maybe these people just don't want to know.

As the author I have interrupted this story from time to time. Anyone who writes a story no doubt has feelings about it. To express them seems quite natural to me. I have felt, in varying degrees, doubt, satisfaction, boredom, lack of confidence, unmitigated enthusiasm and anger. I have also digressed into memories adapted for the page, and unrelated tangential interests or whims. In this way I have become a character in my own story, no more nor less real than any of the other denizens. Scaduto, in her book *Unnoticed Secrets*, seems to postulate that people are parts of the buildings they inhabit. So I am a part of this story. That's the way I interpret it, though maybe she was talking of words not people.

In one of my digressions I referred to Roland Barthes' essay, *The Death of the Author*. Though I cannot claim to be particularly familiar or knowledgeable about his work in literary criticism, or in Structuralism and Post-Structuralism, my interest was aroused by his statement that there are two types of reader—the readerly reader and the writerly reader. The former enjoys books where everything is spelled out. There is no room for interpretation. It is a passive experience. For the latter, reading is a creative process. The writerly reader will create the meaning of the book. An author's biography, intention or meaning have less relevance than the act of creative reading.

I don't necessarily agree or disagree. It is a concept that laps at my ankles. However, I think I have found my own way to a similar place. In this book the characters are fluid. One may create another. A person might be real but also imagined. They all might have been created by the author who also has a role as a fictional being. Different perspectives are seen simultaneously, which is why I called it a cubist biography.

I have come to value what I consider to be honesty in writing. By that I don't mean truth or lies, which are not particularly relevant to fiction. It is more a question of not self-consciously trying to hoodwink a reader for an ulterior motive, which might be no more than the desire for self-aggrandisement. I think perhaps I've been eighty-seven percent successful in that regard, and in this appendix possibly only thirty-two percent. I am not serious about being serious. This will be my last intrusion into your mind for the time being.

Tom Newton

London, 1958

Appendix 2

Unnoticed Secrets

In her book of fourteen essays, *Unnoticed Secrets*, Renata Scaduto (1896-1977) tackled a wide variety of subjects. Among them were included such titles as *Alchemy and the Domestic Kitchen*, *Religion in Stone*, and *Road Building in the Ancient World*. The essay that most appealed to Fabian was *The Game of Opposites*, subtitled: *In Absence there is Presence*.

Scaduto succinctly and very quickly conjured the sense that a universe was encapsulated in a single word. She started traditionally enough with an examination of its etymological origins. Her book was written in Italian and originally published as *Segreti Inosservati* (Bompiani, 1949) but the word 'opposite' has the same Latin root in both Italian and English, as noted by the translator, Elliot Speare. The Latin word in question was the verb *opponere*, and its past participle *oppositus*.

She described the two antagonistic poles of an opposite as sharing the same field—for example hot and cold occupied the field of temperature, close and far of distance, and so on.

The two antagonists created dynamism. Their relationship with the shared field was as if they lived in a building while also being part of its structure. Without it they would have no meaning and without their tension the field could not be defined. There would be no such thing as an opposite, just an infinite homogeneity. The triangular relationship between antagonists and shared field created forces of attraction and repulsion, so in the very meaning of the word opposite, there was another opposite. Recursion was at work.

In this essay, she claimed that the word 'opposite' was a mechanism which generated energy on a subatomic, semantic level. After positing the opposite as a mini power generator, she then asked the question "Why two?" Why were there only two antagonistic poles in an opposite? An affiliation with the number two might seem natural, as the human body is generally equipped with two of most limbs and organs. They provide spare parts in an evolutionary sense and probably aid balance, which would be an advantage in negotiating the physical world. However Scaduto saw it more as involving the time it takes to count. Humans, she said, can quickly recognise a quantity up to four at a glance, without having to calculate. Above that number they need to count. If an opposite consisted of ten different poles, each one equally repelling the others, there would be 1,023 connections between them. She reached this number using the mathematical formula, 2 to the power of n -1. The time it would take to calculate so many possible combinations and appreciate their meaning would be too long to conform to the speed of conversation, or even thought. The relationships contained within such an opposite would be simply too complicated to use.

All of the ideas presented in *Segreti Inosservati* pose the question whether the author wished to be taken seriously or if she was just being satirical. There is some controversy regarding the English edition. Elliot Speare has been criticised for being too free with his translation. Some of his more ardent detractors have questioned how much of *Unnoticed Secrets* was written by Scaduto and how much by Speare himself. They claim it is not the same book.

Scaduto was born Renata Maria Bianchi in 1896, the second of three siblings, and grew up in a working class family in Bologna. At the age of nineteen she married Antonio Scaduto, a violinist at the Teatro alla Scala Orchestra. They took up residence in Milan, where she lived for the rest of her life. For some years she worked in the postal service until she and her husband were blacklisted during the fascist era. After the Second World War she wrote *Segreti Inosservati*, her only published book. She had two sons, Vittorio Francesco and Paulo Lorenzo Scaduto.

Appendix 3

Jaroslav Zlodyk 1913-1976

Jaroslav Zlodyk was born and spent his first years in Dubrovnik. When he was seven, his father, Darko Zlodyk (1885-1963), was offered the Chair of Mathematics at the University of Zagreb and the family moved to that city.

At eighteen Jaroslav also entered the same university to study philosophy but did not complete his degree, changing instead to art. He later credited his mother, Berislava Zlodyk (1887-1971) for this decision. She was a Symbolist painter. He said her example made his future become clear to him—as an artist with a philosophical bent.

The critic Gabriel Channings held that Zlodyk was neither artist nor philosopher. There are only two paintings attributed to him, both in The National Gallery but not currently on display. He never espoused any particular philosophy, and never formulated one of his own. He wrote nothing. He was anything but prolific. Channings regarded him as an impostor and brazen opportunist, an affront to the art world.

In hindsight Zlodyk might be seen as ahead of his time. He stated that one work of art should take a lifetime to complete. It could be that his artwork was his own life and the way he lived it—not a prevalent concept at the time.

He caused a stir when he arrived in England in 1953. He was an imposing figure, eccentric and flamboyant, and could often be seen walking in central London dressed as a Turkish Janissary. He was outspoken and prone to sweeping statements— "There is no such thing as information." The press loved him. He was a sudden incandescence in dreary post-war life.

During the Second World War he had fought as a partisan. A few years later he was smuggled into Austria in an oil drum. From there he was flown to London. In an unusually short time he was granted British citizenship. This caused speculation that he was a British Intelligence asset, and for unknown reasons had been extracted and relocated. Officially it was neither confirmed nor denied. One would assume that such an affair would have been kept secret, but Zlodyk relished talking about how he had entered the United Kingdom in a barrel, even though he had arrived by plane from Vienna.

He had the aura of a new Diogenes, someone wise and contrary. Perhaps to accentuate this image he would wander around with a torch in his hand, apparently looking for something in broad daylight. Soon he was courted by the intelligentsia. He gave up his council flat. For the rest of his life he would be homeless. This may have been his own choice. The reasons are unclear. He never spoke about it. At first he was hosted as a guest by university professors, and moved constantly among them, regaling them with his *zlodykisms*. He claimed to have made time stand still. A claim that at least had some basis to it.

Before the war in Zagreb, he had made a mechanistic sculpture, entitled *Horalogica*—the only object he ever made, or in this case re-engineered. It consisted of a large clock—of the kind found in railway stations. As the hour and minute hands rotated, the clock-face would counter-rotate in perfect synchronisation. The effect would be that time did not advance, even though motion was perceptible. Zlodyk was interested in temporality. He said time was localised in spaces that were immeasurable. You could not know their size. In one place time might stop. In another it might move forward at great speed. Those places might be geographically close to each other. It was all unknowable. Knowledge of it would cause it to lose reality.

Zlodyk would often qualify his declarations with something to the effect that: "it could not be known." His critics were quick to note that this was a cheap way out of the corners he had backed himself into with his nonsensical statements that he could not support with facts.

Horalogica is thought to still exist. It is most likely in a private collection.

Eventually the university professors began to tire of him. They realised he had no intellectual depth, and was never able to back up anything he said with a reasoned argument. He found himself living on the London streets. He was still famous and had many supporters outside the intellectual establishment willing to help him, some of them wealthy. Lord Burnley made him a permanent guest at his country estate in Northumberland. Zlodyk stayed there for just over two years until a disagreement between them ended that arrangement and he was back on the streets, this time in Manchester. The newspapers stopped reporting on him and he disappeared from public view.

He resurfaced in London in 1966, when he was sought out by the avant-garde.

"Nothing can exist without its opposite," he told them. "You can't have electricity without a positive and negative charge."

A group of young artists began to coalesce around him, calling themselves The Friends of Zlodyk. They revered him as an elder statesman of the Absurd, someone who had travelled through exotic mental landscapes.

Though apparently strident, Zlodyk's statements left a lot of room for interpretation. Their ambiguity was a source of inspiration for The Friends of Zlodyk and led to numerous works of art.

The group published a newsletter about once every two months in which they discussed his ideas and introduced works of their own. One issue, which included: *Windows are Important* and *Each Individual is a Museum*, led to the famous Diorama Exhibition at the ICA.

This was an installation by multiple artists. The show was a success, though not as extensive as originally planned, due to cost and limitations of space. There were three large dioramas.

On entering the gallery, a visitor would first encounter *Compulsive Sand*. Its floor sloped gently upwards, covered in sand and scraggly desert plants. The back wall, curved and incorporating the sides, was painted to continue this desert scene in perspective, and was topped with a still, blue sky. It was reminiscent of the dioramas in natural history museums. It had the same air of decay. It looked old but timeless. Nothing moved.

That stillness in museum dioramas, so unnatural to life, negates their attempts at reality. The painstaking attention to detail, the focus on providing the correct flora and fauna for each geographical location, runs counter to the fact that the constructed scene has nothing to do with reality beyond existing. It seems to be in opposition to itself. One wonders about the purpose of these installations. Perhaps their intention is not to portray reality but only its imagining. The spectre of death is omnipresent, for the animals that grace the foregrounds, frozen in rumination and gently staring through the glass, were killed in order to make these displays. There is a decadent aesthetic to it. There is also the element of voyeurism, akin to the old fairground sideshows, where people would gawk at human anomalies. The audience is complicit.

Compulsive Sand was designed to replicate the kind of diorama seen in museums. Most people have viewed dioramas since childhood and therefore have the mental architecture to receive them. As Zlodyk said—"Everything needs somewhere to go—a hat requires a hook." The artists who created the piece clothed their message in the familiar, so it could sneak into the minds of its beholders surreptitiously like a flea on the back of a dog. Once there it would have a subversive and corrosive effect.

The majority of viewers found *Compulsive Sand* to be quite disturbing. Instead of the usual animals there were piles of mannequin parts littered across the landscape. In the foreground was a huge heap of heads, torsos, disconnected hands, and limbs jumbled together with no order, as if they had just been dumped there. Smaller piles receded into the background, conforming to that curious museum diorama perspective, which is not real perspective, which itself is not real either.

On first impression the tangled limbs might have suggested *The Garden of Earthly Delights* but almost immediately the difference became apparent. Bosch was painting the living, whether as corporeal or soul-like, demon or human, heaven or hell. *Compulsive Sand* was about the dead, the devaluation of life, a horrific crime against humanity.

The next diorama, entitled *Art Gallery*, took a completely different approach. Gone were the stillness and the conflict between reality and its representation. There was life and movement. It was constructed to be a mirror image of the gallery showing the exhibition. There were no curved walls or sloping floor. It was exactly the same as the twenty feet of space opposite, separated by the glass, including the bench in the middle of the room. Actors would drift through, pausing to stare at the people on the other side of the glass. They were skilled enough to refrain from any communication, even if there was direct eye contact. It was a delightfully light-hearted play upon perception—who was the observer, who was the work of art?

The last piece, called *Window*, had to be viewed through an orifice. Only one person at a time could look. It simulated the view of an empty street at night, seen from a window high up in a building. The effect was startlingly real, aided by a lens that accentuated distance.

Six dioramas were originally intended but when no more than three were possible, a smaller piece was added. This was *The Rotating Painting*. Zlodyk liked rotation and said that paintings hung in art galleries must turn round (sic). *The Rotating Painting* was an abstract work about three by four feet in dimension. It hung near the exit. Every five minutes the painting would rotate ninety degrees, sometimes clockwise, sometimes anti-clockwise, powered by an electric motor on a timer. It demonstrated how a picture could change depending upon its position, or the position of the viewer.

The exhibition was well received and some of the young artists involved, most notably Brenda Richardson and Terence McNulty, went on to have successful careers. Zlodyk was not involved with the show and made no comment about it, though it was inspired by things he had said, or what The Friends of Zlodyk (since 1968 abbreviated to FOZ) purported him to have said.

Detractors claimed that most of the ideas attributed to Zlodyk had been invented by FOZ who were cynically exploiting a mentally ill, homeless man as a concept for their own artistic conceits. FOZ vehemently denied this accusation.

Zlodyk never married or had children. As far as is known he never had any intimate relationships. As he said: "I was born alone. I will die alone. In meantime I are myself."

Jaroslav Zlodyk died on May 14th, 1976. His body was discovered in the early hours of the morning by dustbin men on Berwick Street in London. His cause of death was listed as heart failure.

FOZ raised money for his funeral and burial. He is interred in Highgate Cemetery, one of his favourite places, not far from Karl Marx's giant head. The epitaph on his gravestone reads: "Rather there than here". It was said to have been chosen by him, but even in his death controversy abounds. There is an opinion that what he actually said was "Rather here than there," and another that the epitaph was written by an FOZ member.

True to his idea about the importance of opposites, Jaroslav Zlodyk was simultaneously both an entity and non-entity, an artist whose influence was larger than himself.

Appendix 4

An excerpt from the new edition of Whereto Fore *by Gustavus Namoor, Pendragon Press, 2024. This excerpt is from the eleventh stanza.*

WHEN THE FIRST CITY WAS BUILT the inhabitants fled. They preferred to live out in the open with their goats as they had always done before. They left their footsteps on the hills as they crossed to the plains beyond. The hills listened and remembered.

I have told you many times
that the thoughts of hills
are egg-shaped
and clandestine.

The king who had founded the city was angry and afraid. Without a population he was powerless. He cursed his guards for neglecting their duty. They wandered off one by one, two by two, three by three, until he was alone among his mud brick buildings.

One day he burst into flames.
His ashes were carried away
By the wind,
And forgotten.

The ashes fell with the rain on to a wheat field and he was consumed as bread by the people who had abandoned him.

Such are the rewards of power.

Appendix 5

Fabian Lear Davis

January 20, 1920 / Staines, UK / 05:47:00 AM GMT
ZONE: + 00:00 / 000W31'00" / 51N26'00"

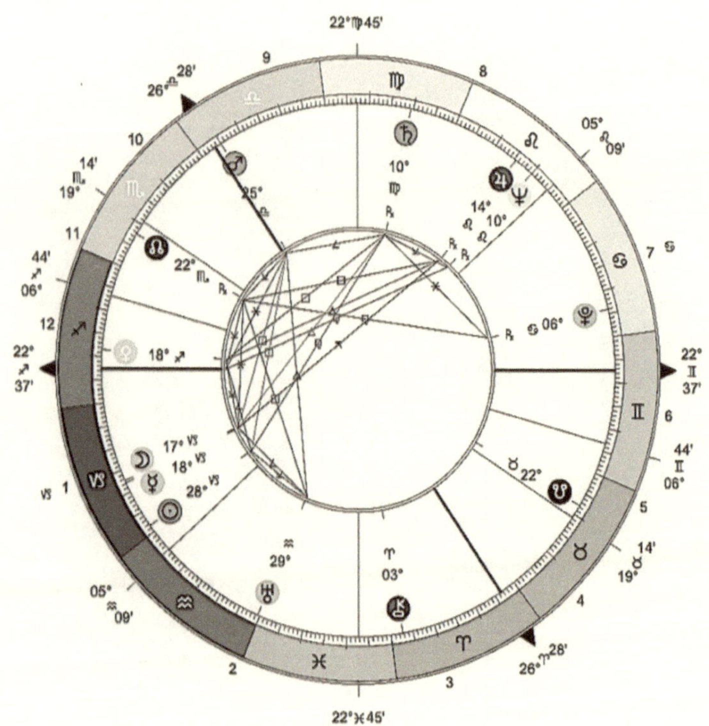

Appendix 6

F ABIÁN D OMINGUEZ

January 20, 1494 / Mérida, Spain / 05:47:00 AM LMT
ZONE: + 00:00 / 006W20'00" / 38N55'00"

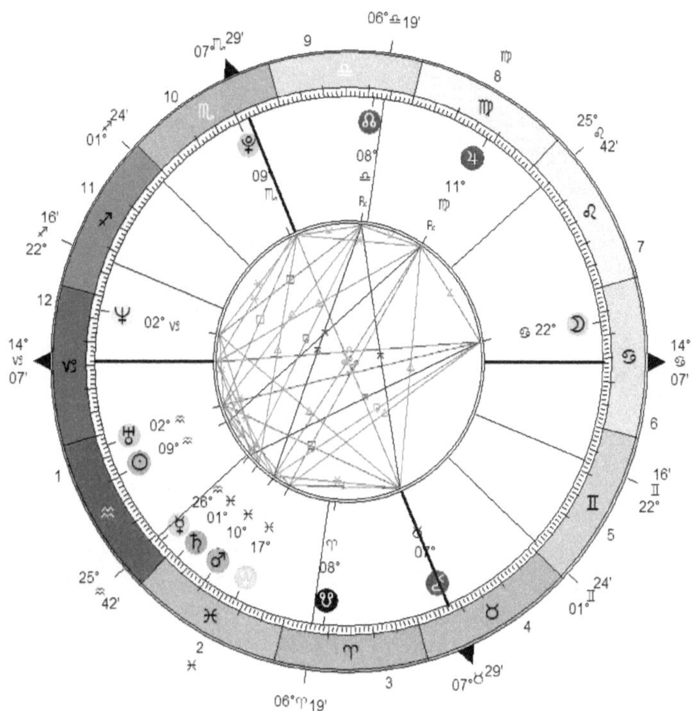

Tom Newton lives in Woodstock, New York with his wife and daughter. His novella *Warfilm* was published by Bloomsbury in 2015. He is the author of *Seven Cries of Delight and Other Stories* (Recital Publishing, 2019) and *Voyages to Nowhere: Two Novellas* (Recital Publishing, 2021).

His interests lie in psychology, art, music, science, mythology, and history.

He spent many years working in the film industry as a prop man, while pursuing a parallel career as a musician and sound engineer. He was a participant in London's punk music scene in the late seventies.

And please check out *The Strange Recital*, a podcast about fiction that questions the nature of reality.